CHRISTMAS IN CAPE MAY

CLAUDIA VANCE

CHAPTER ONE

Margaret and Liz stared up in disbelief at the huge hole in the bathroom's ceiling for a full five minutes. Water leaked everywhere. They hadn't accounted for all these issues when they enthusiastically accepted their Great Aunt Mary and Uncle Lou's offer to take over The Seahorse Inn, a nine-bedroom bed-and-breakfast right on the beach in Cape May, New Jersey.

Not only was there a leaky hole in the ceiling, but they had discovered rotting floorboards in one of the bedrooms, disguised by a queen bed overtop; the basement flooded whenever it rained a lot; the wallpaper in numerous rooms had begun to peel; and the steps leading up to the porch were falling apart. New issues arose every day.

Margaret grabbed a bucket and placed it under the ceiling leak. "I know how to fix some things, but these issues are out of my league."

Liz sighed. "You're telling me. What did we get ourselves into? This place is feeling more and more like a money pit."

It was mid-November, and they had just started working on getting the B&B back up and running again, a task they thought would be a lot easier. It had been years since the place was a functioning B&B, and it showed.

"Hey," a voice said behind them.

Margaret turned around to see Dave standing in the hallway with his bag of tools. "Dave! This place is a mess. We don't even know *what* to do. Thank you so much for coming over."

"Well, I can definitely take a look to see what the issue is," Dave said, setting up a ladder.

Margaret and Liz watched in amazement as he tinkered with the exposed plumbing in the ceiling.

"Yep. That's what I thought. You have a leaking water pipe. I think I can probably fix this right up for you, but before I get to this, show me the other issues in the house," Dave said as he wiped his dirty hands on the rag hanging out of his pocket.

Margaret's heart fluttered whenever she watched Dave work with his hands. He was incredibly skilled and strong.

After walking around the house, inspecting every little issue, Dave referred to his notes, stating, "Most of these issues, I should be able to fix rather quickly, but the basement—I will definitely need help with that."

Margaret looked over at Liz. "OK, but let us pay you. This is way too much work."

"If you just pay for the materials, and my time can be paid for with your delicious meals," Dave said with a wink. "You know me. I love a good project, and I quite enjoy spending time with you, Margaret, so it's a win-win."

Margaret blushed and felt her heart warm. "I can't thank you enough, Dave. I'm going to head back to the living room and get back to working on fundraising for the wildlife refuge. Donations have been coming in steady, and I need to keep on top of it. Let me know if you need anything."

"Yeah, I have to leave to meet up with one of my interior design clients. Thank you, Dave," Liz said as she grabbed her purse and made her way out the door.

Dave stared up at the ceiling and shouted out to Margaret, "You know, I think I can get this all fixed in a little over a week."

"Really?" Margaret said with excitement. "That would work out wonderfully. We've been excited at the thought of having the B&B ready for guests coming to town in December for all of the Christmas festivities."

* * *

With The Cape May Garden Farm Stand closed up for the winter, they now had some extra time to plan out the opening of the B&B.

It was Saturday morning, and Liz and Margaret made plans to meet at the B&B with the kids. The kids kept themselves busy with a stack of board games in the living room while Margaret and Liz brought their laptops to the kitchen table to figure out the *breakfast* part of their bed-and-breakfast.

"I say we have one sweet and savory option every day for breakfast," Liz said while studying menus from other B&Bs in the area.

"That's what I was thinking. We can even change them up to match whatever the season is. Maybe the sweet option in December can be gingerbread or eggnog pancakes," Margaret said while skimming through recipes on her laptop.

Liz started typing a list. "Let's start off with a menu for December since that's when it looks like we'll possibly be ready to open."

"OK, here are some other breakfast ideas for December: frittata, quiche, baked French toast, hash brown casserole, hot sausage and biscuit casserole ..." Margaret had a million breakfast ideas.

Liz couldn't write fast enough. "I think this is plenty for our list for December. Now we need to find some good recipes for

3

these and start doing some test cooking to make sure they are good enough for our guests to eat."

"Did someone say they need a taste tester?" Dave half-joked as he popped his head into the kitchen.

"Oh, we will definitely need your opinion on these breakfast recipes before we open," Margaret said matter-of-factly.

"You can count on me. I got the parts I needed, so I'm going to get back to work on the house, if that's OK," Dave said.

"Of course. Again, we can't thank you enough. I'm going to try one of these recipes today, right after we grocery shop. I'll have it ready for you for lunch."

By the late afternoon, Liz left Margaret and Dave to work in peace, taking all of the kids with her. Margaret had cooked up a storm and Dave had gotten quite a lot of work (and taste testing) done.

Startled by a knock at the door, Margaret opened it to see it was her ex-mother-in-law, Elaine, standing there with a scowl on her face and her purse tightly pressed up in her armpit.

Margaret had never gotten along with Paul's mother. Nothing had ever been good enough for her, including Margaret. They were exact opposites. Elaine was negative about everything, whereas Margaret always tried to see the positive side of things. This ticked off Elaine, and Margaret tried to avoid her whenever possible during her marriage.

"Hi … Elaine? What are you doing here? How did you even know I was here?" Margaret asked, confused.

"I called your mother. She told me you'd be here. I need to speak with you," Elaine said, forcing her way inside before Margaret even had the chance to invite her in.

Margaret was unsure as to why Elaine would have called her mother. They didn't get along either, though they did used to exchange e-mails to talk about their shared granddaughters once in a while.

"Well, it's a nice place you've got here. It's just you running it?" Elaine asked, eyeing the place up and down.

"No. Liz, my sister, and I are both getting the inn up and functioning. Our aunt offered us the place unexpectedly, and we decided to take it on." Margaret looked over at the kitchen to make sure she hadn't missed the oven timer for the latest recipe she was working on.

"Well, I came here to talk about Paul. I know you two are divorced now, but I don't like his new fiancée one bit. That Sandy gal? She's awful."

Margaret sighed. "Elaine, you didn't like me either when I was married to Paul. I think you need to lighten up a little. Also, did you just say fiancée?"

"Yep. That's what I said. *Fiancée*. He popped the question to that dreadful woman, and now I'm beside myself. Also, I never hated you, we just had our differences. You never took my son away from me like *she* has." Elaine's eyes welled up with tears.

"What are you talking about?"

"Well, you know how Paul used to visit his father and I weekly when you two were married? He'd come by every Sunday and sit and talk, sometimes even stay for dinner and help out with small tasks around the house. He hasn't done that in months, and now that his father is gone, it makes that void feel even bigger. He stopped when he starting see *that* woman."

Margaret sighed. "I wouldn't be too concerned, Elaine. He probably stopped because he's in a new relationship. You know how that can be when you start seeing someone new, right? You want to spend every waking minute with them. I wouldn't take it personal. It will pass."

Elaine blew her nose into a tissue she'd pulled from her purse. "I don't think you understand. He won't even return my calls. I haven't even been able to see my granddaughters since you two were divorced. This is not like him, and I think she has some sort of tight, controlling grip on him."

Margaret sighed. "It's interesting, I have noticed he's not spending as much time with the girls either. He's been cancelling plans with them more often, which is out of character for him."

Margaret suddenly felt horrible for Elaine. All of the negative feelings she'd harbored toward her vanished as she poured out her heart and sadness to Margaret.

"Elaine, how about you put your stuff down, and I'll make you a cup of tea. I've got a bunch of food cooking if you're hungry."

Elaine nodded, blotting her eyes again, and took a seat at the kitchen table amid the delicious aroma of baked goods.

"My oh my, it smells wonderful in here. I'll take a piece of whatever you've got," Elaine said a little more cheerfully.

Margaret smiled. "Good, I need more taste testers. We are trying to plan out our breakfast options for when we reopen the B&B. Here's a piece of the hash brown casserole and the fresh cranberry orange pancakes," she said while putting the plates in front of Elaine.

Elaine took a couple of bites and let out a loud groan.

"What? What is it?" Margaret asked, a little worried something was wrong with what she'd cooked.

"Oh, this is the best thing I've tasted in a while. My taste buds are having a dance party right now," Elaine said while dancing her fork in the air.

Margaret laughed.

Then Elaine laughed.

The next thing Margaret knew, they were laughing so hard tears streamed down their faces, and they could barely catch their breath.

Margaret had no idea why it was so funny, but it was. Maybe it was all those pent up emotions towards each other being released. All those years married to Paul, she'd never bonded with Elaine until now, after they were divorced.

"Well, let me get you a cup of tea," Margaret said as she walked over to fill the tea pot on the stove.

"So, Margaret, I know you're not going to get back with my son—as much as I wish you would at this point—however, is there any way you would talk to him? Maybe help him understand how I feel as his mother? He won't even return my calls. I miss my granddaughters dearly and my son. I'm just worried. You're all I've got to get through to him. He doesn't have siblings, and I don't have any of his friends' contact information," Elaine said, turning serious again.

Margaret muddled some lemon in the mug for the tea and looked over at Elaine. "I'm not sure it's my place. And to be frank, I don't really want much to do with him anymore after what he did."

Elaine looked up abruptly at Margaret. "What are you talking about?"

Margaret had let something slip that wasn't meant to get out to her. Sighing, she brought the tea over to Elaine. "I hadn't planned on telling many people this, but when he left for a month without any explanation, I found out he was seeing another woman—Sandy. I had already asked for a divorce prior to knowing this, and decided I was better off not bringing it up to him. He still doesn't know I know. Let bygones be bygones, you know?"

Elaine clenched her teeth. "You've got to be kidding me. He left *you* for *her?* That boy has lost his mind."

"Listen, do not bring this up to him. I don't want him to hear it from you. If it comes from anyone, it will be me. Can you promise me that?" Margaret said with a serious look.

"You've got it, dear. My lips are sealed. In the meantime, can I coordinate seeing my granddaughters with you since my son is of no help with that?"

"Elaine, I'd be happy to have you see them. Just name the place and time. They'd love to see their grandmother."

Elaine jumped out of her seat and threw her arms around

Margaret, squeezing as tight as she could. "You don't even know how much happier I am now. You have made my day."

Suddenly, creaky footsteps ascended from the basement, and both women looked over to see Dave appear.

"Well hello, ladies," Dave said with enthusiasm.

"Elaine, this is Dave," Margaret said matter-of-factly.

Elaine looked over at Dave. He was taller than Paul, and well built, if Margaret did say so herself. He looked quite a bit stronger than Paul. He was attractive with his piercing blue eyes and a head full of thick, wavy salt-and-pepper hair. She looked back at Margaret. "Dave, you say? And *who* is Dave?"

Dave pulled up a chair backwards to the table and straddled it.

"Yeah, who am I, Margaret?" Dave snickered.

Margaret's face was a shade of tomato red at this point. Though she'd started dating Dave back in the summer, she'd never said out loud what he was to her. He had always been introduced as a *friend,* because that's what they were for a while prior.

"Oh, Dave? Yes, Dave. He's a special one, that Dave. We work together at Pinetree Wildlife Refuge and formed a friendship during my divorce proceedings. He's also helping us bring The Seahorse Inn back to life," Margaret said while fiddling with the tablecloth.

"So, in other words, he's your boyfriend?" Elaine asked.

Dave jabbed his finger into Margaret's side to tickle her. "Yeah, am I your *boyfriend?*"

Margaret started hysterically laughing as Dave went into full-blown tickle mode and between each breath of air, she tried to talk. "Yes! Yes! You're my boyfriend. OK? Are you happy? Is that what you wanted to hear?"

Dave stopped tickling her. "Yep, that's all I wanted to hear. First time hearing those words since we started dating. Elaine, you witnessed it. Now I have someone here to vouch for me."

Margaret, still reeling from laughter, felt a little flush of embarrassment by the spectacle taking place in front of Elaine. She wasn't at all sure how Elaine would feel about it.

Elaine had a smile plastered on her face. "Margaret, I don't know if I've ever seen you this happy before. This Dave is good for you. Don't tell my son I told you that though."

"Who's your son?" Dave asked curiously.

"Oh, my son is Margaret's ex-husband, Paul," Elaine said.

Margaret looked over at Dave. "Yeah, I hadn't gotten to that part yet. She's not fond of Sandy, and she's upset that Paul's been MIA lately."

Dave laughed. "Oh, that Sandy. She's a piece of work. She goes through boyfriends faster than anyone I've ever known. Do you know she's been engaged four times in ten years? Gets cold feet, I guess. You'd better tell Paul to watch out. I only know this because she's my ex-wife's best friend."

Elaine looked horrified. "What? You're kidding! Paul already proposed."

"Oh, man. That's not good. Not good at all," Dave said.

Elaine looked back over at Margaret and took her hand. "You're all I've got to knock some sense into him. Please help me. At least for the kids' sake."

Margaret looked over at Dave, who seemed honestly worried about her ex-husband. How amazing it was to be dating someone who didn't seem to have a jealous bone in his body.

"I'll try, Elaine. However, I'm not overstepping my boundaries. I'm going to look at it as helping the girls, like you said." Margaret stood from her chair, smoothing her blouse.

"Thank you. I'd best be going. I'll be in touch about setting up a date to see my granddaughters," Elaine said while standing up and putting her purse back into her armpit.

Margaret walked her to the door. Elaine stopped one more time, looking around the place. "I think I would love to stay here with my sisters once you get the place in working order. Please let me know about the opening date. The food you made was absolutely delicious. I have high hopes for this B&B."

Margaret gave her one last hug, which still felt weird. They had never hugged—not once in fifteen years. How crazy was it that divorce could bring Margaret closer to her ex-mother-in-law?

CHAPTER TWO

About a week later, as Liz painted one of the bedrooms, and Dave was finishing up the last of the repairs, a loud, alarming scream rang out.

Margaret and Dave ran upstairs to find Liz sprawled out on the floor, her left leg mostly swallowed up by the rotted hardwood. If they were to go downstairs, they'd likely see her jean-clad leg dangling from the ceiling. The B&B had more problems than they could keep up with. Dave would no sooner finish something, then another problem arose.

Dave helped hoist Liz's leg out of the hole in the bedroom floor. "I'm starting to think this B&B is too much work for me to handle alone."

Margaret sat down on the floor next to Liz while she rubbed her leg, assuring her sister it was just a little achy and bruised up.

"I think you're right," Margaret said, feeling defeated. "I'm starting to see why Aunt Mary didn't want this place. Thank you for at least trying, Dave. We really appreciate it."

"Do you think that's why Aunt Mary and Uncle Lou gave us this place? I'm surprised they never told us about all the work it needed."

"Who knows. Remember Mom said they only inherited it from Uncle Lou's parents last year. They probably weren't here enough or interested enough to find out what needed to be fixed." Margaret stared at the hole in the floor.

"You might be right. Mom said Aunt Mary doesn't like the beach. Didn't this place get to be too much for Uncle Lou's parents?" Liz asked.

Margaret sighed. "Yeah. I think they were too old and fragile to really keep it up by the time they gave it to Aunt Mary and Uncle Lou. It may have been many years before anything was repaired here if we hadn't taken it on."

Dave suddenly got a bright idea. "Look, I have some buddies, and possibly my brother, who can help me out. I can ask my friend that has a construction business to come take a look and see if he can find any other major issues."

"You don't have to do all that, Dave. I feel like we're asking too much of you at this point," Margaret said.

Liz stood up abruptly. "How about we make this a family affair? We get everyone involved. It's almost Thanksgiving weekend, and all of the Christmas festivities will have already started in Cape May. We can make this a fun holiday weekend. We can cook some big meals to offer to family and friends who come over and help clean, paint, tear down old wallpaper, fix things, build things, all of that! We can even decorate the Seahorse for Christmas together. They can stay in the rooms that are deemed fit and safe if they want. If we can make that happen, in addition to what Dave has in mind, I think it might just work."

Margaret bit her lip and thought. "It would be amazing if we can get this place ready for bookings by early December."

Liz grabbed Margaret's hand. "Let's go get to work calling and e-mailing friends and family. We should also post an event on social media to reach everyone."

Margaret was skeptical. "I sure hope this works, sister."

* * *

By the next day, they'd received many positive replies to their e-mails and calls about helping with the B&B. The event that Margaret posted on social media, which made cleaning and repairing a B&B seem fun and exciting, showed a lot of family and friends responding. They had about twenty people, including Dave and his buddies, coming over in six days.

"Oh, wow. This is exciting. Having a bunch of our family and friends over to laugh, enjoy each other's company, and work towards one common goal together. I didn't think many people would be interested in helping, but I'm shocked. We need to get to the grocery store now so we can feed everyone. I say we do a Thanksgiving Day spread. It will be like a Friends-giving except with family too."

Margaret clasped her hands together. "I'm loving this idea, Liz."

As Liz and Margaret walked out to the car, one of the B&B owners next door looked over at them from the porch.

"Oh, look—it's one of our neighbors. We've been so busy trying to fix up this B&B that we've neglected to introduce ourselves to the them," Margaret told her sister before raising her voice and waving to their neighbor. "Hi, I'm Margaret and this is Liz, my sister."

The woman scowled, dumped what was left of her coffee into the bushes below, turned around, and walked back inside, slamming the front door behind her.

"What was *that* all about?" Liz asked, astonished.

"That was pretty odd. Maybe she didn't see us?" Margaret pondered.

They shrugged it off, hopped in the car, and drove to the local grocery store. They had many mouths to feed this weekend and no time to worry about an unfriendly neighbor.

Once at the store, they each grabbed a cart. The sisters

meal and snack planned on the fly, having a ball and enjoying a nice break from painting and cleaning.

When a man in his sixties stopped his cart right in front them, Liz was a little creeped out. "Why do I know you two? Wait a minute. I've seen you going in and out of the Seahorse. Is that correct?"

"Um … yes. Can I ask how you know that?"

"Oh, I'm John. Your next-door neighbor. I've been wanting to introduce myself, but every time I've gone over, you've already left for the day. I've seen a fella over there too, but he always seems super busy."

Margaret smiled. "So nice to meet you, John. I'm Margaret and this is my sister, Liz. The man you see over there is Dave. We recently were given the B&B from our aunt and uncle. Which house do you live in?"

John pushed his cart to the side of the aisle so people could get by. "Oh, I'm your neighbor on the right, in that purple house. It's home away from home for my wife, Rose, and I. We're retired and live about an hour and half from here. We come down during the summer and on the weekends, usually. Sometimes we'll spend holidays here. It's a wonderful place."

Margaret loved this neighbor already. The happiness and positivity in his voice was enough to make her want to make this B&B work. "That's wonderful, John. We're both from Cape May and love it here too. We're working hard to get the B&B back up and running. We would love for you two to come over sometime for a visit. Say, do you know anything about the neighbor on our left?"

John's smile immediately left his face. "That's Hugh and Betty. Yeah, they run a B&B there. Morning Dew Cottage, I think it's called. They are not the nicest neighbors I've ever had," he said with one loud laugh.

"That's funny because as we were leaving to come here, we waved to the woman and introduced ourselves and she ignored us and walked away," Liz said.

John shook his head. "Yep. That seems about right. They aren't very friendly people, at least to Rose and I. They especially hated the couple who ran your place for many years."

"My Uncle Lou's parents? Are you talking about Henry and Barbara?" Margaret asked.

"Yep. Henry and Barbara. Wonderful people. I miss them. The wife and I would go over to visit them on the porch and have tea or coffee, listen to the ocean while watching the sunrise. They'd be up super early in the morning just like us. Anyway, as I was saying, Henry and Barbara didn't get along with those neighbors and it became an all-out war at one point."

Margaret was shocked by all this drama. "Why exactly was there all this animosity?"

"Well, I never got the full story of what happened. Henry and Barbara didn't like to talk about it much. We had just bought our place next door the year it all started. From what I heard, there'd been an argument and it evolved into a rivalry. They both ran B&Bs, and the Seahorse became more successful for some reason. They may have marketed better? Who knows, really. All I know is they didn't get along at all. Hugh and Betty became spiteful, jealous competitors. Pretty juvenile, if you ask me."

Liz's mouth dropped open. "You're kidding."

"Oh, I kid you not. Word was Hugh and Betty were badmouthing the Seahorse to all of the people who stayed at their B&B. One time, Henry caught Hugh dumping his grass clippings and leaves over the fence into their yard. It's like they were trying to sabotage their business and make their lives miserable. The kicker was when the police got called. You know how street parking can be pretty hard to find in these parts? Well, it can be a little hard for the B&B guests to find parking during the busy season. Hugh and Betty sneakily told their guests to park in the Seahorse's driveway one morning when Henry and Barbara briefly left before their guests arrived. They came back to find their driveway full to the brim, and not one spot available for any of their guests."

"Well, that explains it then. They aren't happy about us possibly reopening the place," said Margaret matter-of-factly.

"Nothing like a nightmare neighbor on top of the money pit," Liz said shaking her head.

John immediately piped up. "Now, now. I didn't mean to scare you two. We are elated that someone is *finally* bringing the Seahorse back to life. That place has been vacant for a long time, aside from Mary and Lou and their friends coming by once in a blue moon the past year, but I don't really count that."

"Well, it was great meeting you John, and thank you for filling us in. We will surely see you around."

Margaret shook his hand, and they made their way around the rest of the grocery store, stocking up on all of the items needed to feed everyone for the weekend with just a little more skepticism about this B&B than before.

By the time they got back, Dave was already working, having just arrived after his shift at the Pinetree Wildlife Refuge, and they filled him in on the neighbor drama.

"You're kidding me. Who knew the B&B business could be so scandalous?" Dave said with a booming laugh.

"Yeah, it looks like we have some relationships to repair around here, if possible. It doesn't sound like Uncle Lou's parents were in the wrong, but who knows what the whole story is," Margaret said while putting groceries away.

"'Repair'? I don't know about that. Not sure I want anything to do with those people. They seem very spiteful. I don't want that negativity around me or our guests," Liz said sternly.

"I guess we'll just see what happens." Margaret tried to stay somewhat optimistic.

* * *

The next day, Paul picked Harper and Abby up after school and took them out for pizza and a movie. When he dropped them off at the B&B, he didn't have Sandy with him for once. He walked the girls up the steps to the front door, seeing the Seahorse for the first time.

Margaret stepped outside to grab the girls' backpacks. "Well, did you have a good time, girls?"

"Yes! We got pizza and saw that movie—you know, with the cartoon dinosaur?" Abby said.

Margaret didn't have a clue what movie she was talking about but pretended she did.

The girls got a glimpse of Dave inside, screeched with excitement, and ran through the door. "Hi, Dave!"

Paul just rolled his eyes. He didn't love that his daughters loved Dave.

It was just Margaret and Paul standing outside on the porch, so she figured the ideal opportunity had presented itself.

"Well, I guess I'll be going. Sandy's waiting at home for me," Paul said, sounding exhausted.

"Hey, Paul ... I've been meaning to talk to you about something. Your mom came to talk to me last week about you," Margaret said.

Paul's eyes widened in disbelief. "My mom? Came to talk to you? About me? Well, that's shocking. What could she have possibly wanted to talk about?"

"She's upset that you haven't visited or returned her calls in months. She says it's not like you. She felt that I was the best way to get through to you."

Paul sighed. "I know. I feel horrible about it. It's not what I want. It's just ..."

"It's just what, Paul? Please tell me you're not allowing Sandy to call the shots about when you can see or talk to your mother or even your daughters. I've noticed you've been canceling more often when you're supposed to be with the girls."

Paul immediately got defensive. "No, that's not it at all. We've just been … busy."

Margaret could tell that was a lie. "Paul, you know that I know that you went away that month to be with Sandy, right?"

Paul was unprepared for where the conversation was headed. "I … um … No, I didn't know that."

Margaret crossed her arms. "I had already asked for a divorce before I found out so I never brought it up. But I knew you were having an affair, and I knew that nonsense you made up about being alone and connecting with your deceased dad that whole month away was a lie."

Paul stared at his feet unable to find any words.

Margaret grew red with annoyance. "Look, it is what is. We're divorced, and I've moved on, and it appears you have too. However, please don't neglect your Mom. She loves you. She isn't going to be here forever, and she wants to see you and her granddaughters. Elaine told me she hasn't seen Harper or Abby in months. She's now coordinating with me to see them instead. *Me.* The person she never got along with is now the person she is seeking out."

Paul was silent, then cleared his throat. "You know when that call came to the house when I was away for a month and the girls picked it up? Then the person hung up?"

Margaret nodded.

"Well, that was me. I'd started to have second thoughts about everything with Sandy. I missed the girls. I missed you. I was alone in the bedroom and decided to call, but as soon as the girls picked up, Sandy walked in the room, and I had to hang up," Paul said shaking his head.

Margaret said nothing and stared at him while shaking her head.

Paul continued on. "That night of the storm, I had completely changed my mind about everything. I wanted to amend our marriage. I wasn't ready to tell you the truth about everything just yet for fear that you would end it all. But then you did end it all the next morning when you asked for a divorce. I didn't really it show it, but I was in shambles. At that point, I only had Sandy to turn to for support. And well, she made me happy at my lowest point, and it just ended up working out. Then I proposed."

Margaret couldn't believe he was dishing all of this out now, on the front steps of the B&B. "Look, Paul. I'm not sure I need to know all this. However, I really think you need to make some better decisions. Please give your mother a call when you leave here and stop canceling time with your daughters."

Dave popped his head out the door, looked at Paul and nodded, then turned to look at Margaret. "Hey, Liz made dinner for us whenever you're ready to eat."

"Thanks, Dave. I'll be right in," Margaret said with a smile.

She looked back over at Paul who had rolled his eyes. "Dave has been doing amazing work to this B&B, and the girls absolutely love him. You shouldn't be so judgmental. He's a great guy."

Paul was silent and stared at his feet again. He definitely appeared jealous of Dave. Maybe it was because Margaret had this wonderful guy and Paul had a woman who controlled his every move, but he'd never admit that. Maybe he saw everything he was missing out on because of the affair he'd had.

"Look, Paul. I have to get inside. I don't hate you. I sincerely wish you happiness. However, I really think you need to stop ignoring your mother and start taking better control of your own life," Margaret said as she turned to go inside. She was trying to be vague about Sandy.

"I'm perfectly happy, thank you. I'll get in touch the next time I have the girls," Paul said, turning to walk to the car.

As he made his way down the steps, looking depressed, it was obvious he wasn't happy. Margaret could see it plain as day, and she couldn't believe she felt sorry for the man who'd cheated on her and abandoned his daughters for a month without so much as a goodbye.

Margaret walked inside, greeted by a delicious-smelling kitchen and Dave and Liz sitting at the table with full plates waiting for her.

"Jeez. You were out there forever it seemed. We're starving," Liz said sarcastically.

Dave pulled out the chair for Margaret and smiled at her. "I poured you some iced tea."

Margaret smiled back at him. While she'd been on the porch for what seemed like an hour with her ex-husband, Dave had been working on their B&B before pouring her a glass of iced tea and holding dinner for her. He didn't have any insecurities about anything it seemed. Even the nicest of guys would have felt a little tinge of jealousy. Not him. He was a confident man, and Margaret absolutely loved that.

CHAPTER THREE

It was Thanksgiving Day, and Liz and Margaret were at their parents' house to celebrate. Liz's husband Greg, along with Dave, all their the kids, some aunts, uncles and a few cousins were also in attendance. Their mom, Judy, loved to make a big feast for Thanksgiving every year. Everyone who came brought a dish to share, and it ended up being enough food to feed an army. Bob, their dad, had the football game on in the other room, and the kids hung out together, playing games in the back room. This particular Thanksgiving was extra exciting with the B&B about to reopen and a big friends-and-family group effort going on over the long weekend.

Judy laid out a buffet of food, and everyone formed a line to pile their dishes high with turkey, ham, sweet potato casserole, green bean casserole, pineapple stuffing, regular stuffing, mashed potatoes, macaroni and cheese, and the rest of the beloved traditional dishes.

Extra tables and chairs had been placed in the living room since there wasn't enough room at the big dining room table for everyone. The kids had their own little table as well.

Aunt Linda sat next to Margaret and Liz. "I'm so excited

to come help out at the B&B this weekend," she said as she took a bite.

"Oh, that's wonderful. We weren't sure if anyone would really be interested in helping but figured we'd make it a fun family get-together. We're shocked by how many people are coming," Margaret said, sipping her wine.

Aunt Linda reached over for a roll out of the bread basket. "Well, you know I'm pretty good at painting rooms, and your Uncle Mike used to work in construction eons ago. He definitely knows a thing or two."

"I forgot about that. We probably have a bunch of people coming who have some good experience or insight for us," Liz said optimistically.

By the time everyone had finished eating and chatting, Margaret and Liz helped Judy clean up and put out the desserts: pumpkin pie, pecan pie, key lime pie, cheesecake, cookies, and a few other delectable treats.

Dave and Greg were deep in conversation while watching the football game in the other room, and everyone seemed happy and relaxed.

After dessert, it was tradition to walk around the neighborhood and say hi to neighbors. They would bundle up and venture off into the crisp weather to walk off their full tummies, and would usually stop at the nearby playground to let the kids play for bit. The familiarity of their traditions created a warmth that radiated from the inside out for Margaret.

* * *

Friends and family pulled in, one after the other, their cars lining the Seahorse's driveway. Luckily, it was off season so there was plenty of street parking for those who couldn't fit in the driveway.

Margaret and Liz had already tidied up the rooms that would have people staying in them over the weekend. The friends and family who were local would come and go as their schedules allowed; some were only able to help out one day, but most were able to commit to the whole weekend.

The pair stood on the front porch, greeting everyone as they came in. Uncles and cousins brought their huge tool bags with them, ready to get down to business. Friends and relatives arrived bearing home-cooked food dishes, which was unexpected—they hadn't asked anyone to do that. This truly was a family affair, they had a ton of food piled up in the kitchen. A craft station had been assembled in the dining room for the kids, and of course, Bob had college football blaring loudly in the living room for all who cared to peek in and watch.

Their friend Sarah arrived last, bringing with her a man. Margaret and Liz were shocked as she was notorious for being single.

"Hey, everyone. This is Mark," she said excitedly, waving to everyone in the family.

"Well, that was vague," Liz chuckled.

"Yeah, we need the scoop later on this Mark guy," Margaret said.

Dave, a few of his buddies, his brother, and a friend who owned a small construction company were already working in the house, having arrived early to get a head start on the day.

Dave approached Margaret as she organized all of the food, his familiar, low-pitched timbre caused her to smile regardless of the topic. "Hey, so should I show everyone what needs to be done? Maybe we can figure out who is better at what and divvy it up that way?"

"That sounds great. We'll get the kids settled with the crafts and start preparing food for lunch," Margaret said.

Within an hour, everyone was situated with their assigned task and all that could be heard was banging coming from every direction in the house. Aunt Debbie peeled off wallpaper in the living room, Uncle Mike repaired the upstairs floor in one of the bedrooms, some friends painted bedrooms, Uncle Phil was outside repairing the porch and steps, and so on. By the sound of the laughter and talking, everyone was enjoying themselves.

For lunch, Liz and Margaret set out a large spread of some of the dishes that were brought plus some of their own recipes that they were trying out for the B&B menu. Folks were clearly starving, having worked up an appetite, and scarfed most of it down while savoring a nice moment of relaxation and conversation.

After lunch, it was back to the noisy business of progress with a chorus of loud bangs coming from every room. Margaret and Liz helped pull wallpaper down in the foyer and living room while Judy organized dinner preparations.

Liz scraped the wallpaper off with a putty knife in the foyer, then stopped to inspect it. "How many layers of wall paper is there exactly?

Aunt Debbie and some aunts chuckled from the living room. "It seems about six layers so far. It's like a fun surprise each time we get to a new layer," Aunt Debbie said as she continued to work.

Bob, having heard the conversation, poked his head in the living room. "Is that a sailboat wall paper print you've got there? I've got plenty of nautical items to complement it if you decide to keep it."

Margaret chuckled. "Dad, *all* of the wallpaper is going away. We're going to paint the walls. Plus, doesn't Mom like having all of those thrifted nautical things all over the house?".

Judy laughed, having heard the conversation from the kitchen. "No Margaret, I want you to have *all* of our nautical items. They would surely fit in better here. It would give me more room to put my *own* decorations up."

Margaret chuckled at the thought of having wooden fish and nets displayed all over the B&B. While nautical items were appealing as beach decor, it wasn't the aesthetic they were going for.

A few more hours passed by of fixing up the B&B. By dinnertime, mostly everyone had showered and washed the paint and dust off themselves, seizing the opportunity to get into fresh clothes. Some had even run home to freshen up before coming back for dinner. Judy had cooked up a storm and made a wonderful meal of sautéed green beans with shallots, mashed potatoes, ham, and sweet potatoes with some freshly baked biscuits.

Afterwards, Dave pulled Margaret and Liz aside. "So, I went around and looked at today's progress, and am floored. I think this B&B will definitely be ready to reopen the first week of December. Everything is practically done. All of the peeling wallpaper has been removed, the rooms are repainted, all of the floorboards have been repaired. All the other stuff looks to be finished too. This was a great idea getting everyone involved."

Margaret and Liz clasped their hands together and squealed.

"This is so exciting. I'll set up the projector in the living room and put on a movie so everyone can relax. We'll get the desserts out too," Liz said.

After everyone found a comfortable seat in the living room with their dessert, Margaret and Liz made an announcement, drinks in hand. "We just want to thank every one of you for coming this weekend and helping out with getting the Seahorse ready. It looks like we finished ahead of schedule. You all knocked it out of the park today—we are finished! If you'd like to come back tomorrow, we will be decorating for Christmas. We have some ideas up our sleeves to get us all in the Christmas spirit tomorrow too. I think it'll be a lot of fun. So, let's raise our glasses ... cheers to all of us!" Margaret said joyfully.

Everyone hooted and hollered, raising their glasses to clink with those nearby in a toast.

"We would absolutely love to help decorate for Christmas tomorrow," Aunt Debbie said.

Everyone else was pretty excited to help out with the decorating too. Margaret and Liz finally felt the Christmas spirit. It was such a cheerful and cozy time of the year to be opening the B&B.

* * *

The next morning, Liz and Margaret prepared a big breakfast full of many different recipes they'd be using on the B&B menu. The house was loud and joyful, and Margaret tuned the radio to a station that played Christmas music twenty-four seven. It was really starting to feel like that magical time of year.

"You all enjoy breakfast while Liz, Greg, Dave and I run out to get a bunch of Christmas decorations," Margaret said.

"I think we need to take two cars so it can all fit," Liz said eyeing her little sedan.

"Yeah, you're probably right," Margaret agreed.

"Let's use my truck. There's plenty of room in the back," Dave said as he unlocked the doors.

Just as Margaret got to the truck, she noticed Betty, the grouchy neighbor again staring at them from her porch.

Margaret tried to be friendly again. "Hello."

This time the woman answered back, "I hope you're not taking all this parking out front. We need some for our guests, you know."

Margaret was taken aback. *This* was the first thing Betty chose to say to her? After talking to John at the market, she wasn't *that* surprised by this encounter, but it still was shocking nonetheless.

"No. Not at all," Liz said sternly, then slammed her car door before Margaret could get a word out. Liz didn't have any patience for rude people, whereas Margaret tried to give people the benefit of the doubt.

Not wanting to let that little encounter dampen their excited moods, they let it go, and followed each other to the store. Once at the store, they grabbed tons of white string lights, battery-operated candles for the windows, Christmas garlands, wreaths, swags, and everything in between.

"How about we get a couple of small artificial trees for around the house and set up a main tree in the foyer since it has high ceilings. That one could be a big, live tree, and guests would be greeted with the smell of fresh pine as they walk in," Margaret said to Liz.

"Oh, I like that idea. What if we made the Christmas trees different themes? We could do this artificial white tree in a beach theme and put it in the dining room," said Liz while hoisting the huge Christmas tree box onto her cart.

"That's a great idea. How about a rustic tree with a woodland creature theme? I feel like it'll pay homage to the wildlife refuge. Maybe it will start conversations with guests and make them want to follow Pinetree's Facebook page or go visit the refuge," Margaret said while running her fingers over the needles of the display tree.

Greg chuckled and pointed to an aisle across from them. "I think I see ornaments over there that fit both of those Christmas tree ideas."

Dave arrived with a carrier full of hot coffee drinks. "I got us all some fancy gingerbread coffees with whipped cream to get us into the mood while we shop."

Thankful and elated, since there hadn't been much time before they'd left to drink a full cup of coffee, the group collectively sighed while savoring a little quiet time together.

A couple hours—and many shopping carts later—they had procured a ton of Christmas decorations. When they pulled back up to the B&B, some of their friends and family were bundled up and nestled into the rocking chairs on the porch, enjoying the cool ocean breeze with their coffees, while others were inside watching football with Bob.

Sarah and Mark, having gone home yesterday evening, pulled up right as they started to unload the cars.

"Well, well. When are we going to get the full introduction?" Margaret said to Sarah as she motioned to Mark.

Mark laughed. "We actually knew each other back in college and reconnected after bumping into each other at a little coffee shop in the city last month. Funny thing was, we found out we both lived near Cape May."

Sarah chuckled. "I think I was afraid of jinxing anything, so I didn't tell anyone."

Mark smiled and grabbed her hand. "I don't think you have anything to worry about."

Sarah blushed and turned to Margaret and Liz. "Let us grab some of this stuff. Wow. Looks like you really went all out."

Margaret went to grab the big Christmas tree, but Dave put his hand on her back. "Hey, you. I can get that," he said as he hoisted the huge box over his shoulder and proceeded up to the front steps.

Margaret had a moment of warmth and happiness. She watched as the great guys she, her sister, and her best friend had in their lives dutifully and cheerfully unloaded the vehicles.

Once inside, the Christmas music, still going loud and strong, ensured everyone was feeling festive enough to decorate. They were also caffeinated, so that didn't hurt either.

Dave and his buddies tackled the outside and with the help of some extension ladders, cables, and staple guns. They were ready to make the B&B seen from outer space, but in an elegant way. They started at the top of the tallest peak, stapling the string lights along the outline of the Victorian roof.

Down below on the porch, a bunch of aunts and uncles fluffed the swags and garlands, wiring and stapling them along the porch beams, railing, and under the windows. Inside, the kids, Liz, and some friends put together the large artificial trees before decorating them by theme. The entire place was abuzz and joyful.

The weather had started to turn from crisp to cold, and Margaret and Greg decided it was a good idea to get the living room fireplace going. Aunt Mary had said they'd recently had it cleaned out and serviced, so it was good to go. They started the fire, and the house warmed up immediately. The crackle and pops made for such a relaxing environment. Aunt Debbie nailed up a swag adorned with white lights right over the fireplace, and it looked beautiful. Margaret walked over to the many unused tapered ivory candles sitting in the vintage brass holders on the mantle and lit them one by one.

Judy and some aunts organized lunch, another buffet-style feast full of some of Judy's famous creations and some more recipes from the Seahorse menu. Between the fire and the wonderful food, the B&B smelled divine.

Margaret hollered up to the guys on the roof, and everyone else, that lunch was ready. Within minutes, people were scattered throughout the house eating the delicious food. Margaret cut a thick slice of Judy's famous cranberry orange walnut bread and put a big dab of butter on it. It was one of her favorite things her mother made this time of year.

Dave and his friends finished their meals fast so they could try and finish before it got dark outside. This time of the year, daylight was pretty scarce, getting dark right around supper time. They'd finished outlining the peaks of the steeply pitched gable roof and made their way to the trim above the doors on the porch. It looked spectacular already.

Along the wrought iron fence, Margaret and Liz hung long

strands of garland and more white lights. Some cousins put the batteries in the candles before placing one in each window and adding more garland, lights, and decorations on the banister and along the interior door trims.

The sun began its descent toward the horizon, and it would be dark pretty soon. Dave had turned off all of the lights to make for a grand reveal. Everyone gathered, bundled up in coats and hats with hot cider in hand, courtesy of Judy and the aunts. Right as darkness fell, Dave hit the switch and the house lit up like a Christmas tree. The lights were strung perfectly, outlining the entire B&B and showcasing its beautiful Victorian peaks. It looked absolutely marvelous.

For dinner, and to take a break from all of the cooking, Judy made reservations at a local inn's restaurant only a few short blocks away. Though they were a large party, the inn had the perfect setup to accommodate them. Everyone cleaned up, relaxed a little by the fire, and then they all walked over. Once inside, the entire place was also magnificently decorated for Christmas. There were lit candles around the inn with dim, romantic lighting, and elaborately decorated Christmas trees and swags everywhere. They were led to a back room, which they had all to themselves.

Once inside the private room, Margaret and Liz immediately saw Aunt Mary and Uncle Lou already sitting at the table.

"Aunt Mary! Uncle Lou! What are you two doing here?" Liz said joyfully. Margaret ran over to hug them, as did everyone else.

"Well, Judy told me about everything going on this weekend, and since we couldn't make it over to help, we thought we'd treat everyone to a special dinner here at our favorite place to eat in Cape May," Aunt Mary said while still hugging different relatives.

"I kept it a surprise as they asked me to," Judy said with a chuckle.

Servers arrived with plates of appetizers that Aunt Mary had preordered for the table: bruschetta, stuffed mushrooms, sautéed artichoke hearts, freshly baked bread, romaine salad, and oysters.

Drinks and meals were ordered, and everything was delicious. Everyone thanked Aunt Mary and Uncle Lou, who had to get back home, and the group, full of laughs, walked back to the B&B with full bellies.

CHAPTER FOUR

Margaret and Liz stared at their laptop screens as they sat sipping hot mulled cider in the kitchen of the B&B. It was the first week of December, and the Seahorse had been fully cleaned up, repaired, and decorated. They'd put the word out that they were open as best they could and awaited the stampede of bookings … but they only heard crickets. This venture was proving to be costly, and they needed to start bringing guests in as soon as possible if they wanted to make a profit.

They both felt discouraged since they thought for sure regulars who used to stay there years ago would be knocking down the doors to stay again. That just wasn't the case.

Margaret juggled being a newly single mom, working her full-time job, and then with getting the Seahorse up and running, something had to give. She was grateful to have Liz, but her sister had her own juggling to do. They each had full plates, but the B&B was a passion project.

"I feel like we didn't think this through enough," Liz said, closing her laptop.

Margaret took a sip of her cider and leaned back in her chair. "It's too bad this B&B didn't come with an instruction manual. Remember John said that the Seahorse used to be successful? Maybe he and his wife could offer some insight? I really don't want to bother Uncle Lou's parents with these questions. I heard they're both not doing too well right now, and we barely know them. It just seems like too much."

Liz bit her lip and opened her laptop back up. "Maybe Aunt Mary or Uncle Lou might know something? I can e-mail them."

"No, they don't know much. I asked Mom. Aunt Mary never asked questions since she didn't get along with them, and according to Uncle Lou, his parents never talked about their B&B business. They were pretty private people. It makes sense, I guess."

Moments later, the front door opened and Dave strolled in carrying his tool bag. It was Monday and his day off, but he'd become enamored with working on the B&B and was there whenever he could be. He even worked nights after Margaret and Liz went home sometimes.

"Hey, you two," Dave said joyfully.

"Hey, Dave," the sisters said in unison.

"What are you still working on? I thought everything was finished last week," Margaret asked curiously.

"Well, you know old houses. I keep finding little things here and there. Right now, I'm tweaking a few things in the basement," Dave said as he looked over at Liz and winked his eye.

Margaret got a little suspicious. "Oh, what are you working on down there?"

Liz immediately piped up. "Just fixing some lights and stuff. You know how basements can be ...."

"How come you know this and I don't?" Margaret asked.

"Oh, um, well because ... Greg was helping Dave, and he told me."

Dave stood chuckling at their exchange.

"OK, well I want to see it," Margaret said.

"Nope! You will have to wait, and that's an order," Liz said seriously.

Margaret laughed. "OK, fine, but I don't see why I have wait to see a light, but whatever."

Dave hugged Margaret, helped himself to some of the mulled cider on the stove, and made his way down to the basement. Meanwhile, Liz put her coat on.

"Where are you going?" Margaret asked.

"I'm going over to John and Rose's house next door to invite them over. They said they used to be friends with Uncle Lou's parents, so if anyone knows anything, it's gotta be them," Liz said as she wrapped a scarf around her neck.

"Well, wait for me. I'm going too," Margaret said as she quickly grabbed her coat and headed out the door, hot on her sister's heels.

Within fifteen minutes, they were back inside the Seahorse, and John and Rose were elated to be invited over to discuss the B&B. They were due to be over for some snacks and conversation by the fireplace in a half hour.

Margaret and Liz quickly tidied up their work station in the kitchen and whipped up some light snacks. Margaret made a cheese board while Liz threw together some deviled eggs with the hardboiled eggs in the fridge.

John and Rose arrived right on time, and once they walked in, their mouths dropped open.

"Wow! The inside is even more beautiful than when we last saw it," Rose said as she eyed the room.

"She isn't lying. You two have done a terrific job here. Heck, now we want to stay here and we already live next door," John joked.

Margaret took their coats and directed them to the seating area by the fire in the living room. "I'm so glad you two could come over. We opened for business this week, but haven't had one single booking inquiry yet. I know it will take time, and that we should be patient, but we're feeling pretty discouraged at the moment."

Rose immediately piped up. "Oh, you won't have any problems booking this beautiful place. You know, Barbara had a huge guest book full of all the guests who used to stay here. They would fill in their address, phone number, and e-mail. She showed it to me one time. It was full to the brim. She ended up buying multiple books because she had so many interested customers. Have you found them?"

"We wish!" Liz said as she brought out the snacks and placed them on the coffee table.

"We had twenty-five or so people over Thanksgiving weekend cleaning, repairing, and decorating, and nobody found anything like that unfortunately," Margaret said.

"This week we are going to focus on working on the website and the social media page for the Seahorse, and hopefully, that will help some," Liz said optimistically.

"I'll tell you. These snacks are delicious and this house is more wonderfully decorated for the holidays than I've ever seen it. If Henry and Barbara made it a successful business, you two surely will," John said with a smile.

John and Rose stayed for a couple of hours to chat, and Liz and Margaret grew even more fond of them. They were such nice people. They left right around 3 p.m., which gave Margaret and Liz a little extra time to brainstorm together before heading home to their families for dinner.

"I'm going to walk around upstairs and see if I can find these guest books anywhere. I'm sure past guests would love to know about the reopening," Margaret said as she made her way up the staircase.

"Great. I'll stay down here and look," Liz said.

Within fifteen minutes, Margaret called out for Liz. "Can you come up here for a minute?"

Liz immediately went upstairs to where Margaret's voice was coming from. "What's up?"

"Well, I opened the medicine cabinet and found this skeleton key sitting in it by itself," Margaret said holding up the old key.

Liz took the key from her to study it. "All of the doors have modern locks now. I haven't seen anything that would work for this, have you?"

"Nope. Maybe Dave knows. He did a lot of work in these rooms," Margaret said she walked downstairs to call him.

"Hey, Dave," Margaret hollered down through the loud bangs coming from the basement. "Can you come up here for a second?"

The banging stopped, and Dave made his way to the bottom of the basement stairs, dust caked on his hat and clinging to the longish hair curling out around its edges.

Margaret laughed when she saw him. "Wow, you're really getting serious down there, aren't you?"

"You could say that," he confirmed with a smile.

"Do you mind coming upstairs for a minute? We found a key and were curious if you saw something that it might belong to."

Once upstairs, Dave studied the key. "I haven't seen many things this key would work with. There is one place I haven't been in this house yet, though," Dave said as he looked up at the ceiling.

"The attic!" Margaret and Liz both yelled out with excitement.

Out in the hallway, Dave tried to pull down the attic ladder out of the ceiling. It wouldn't budge. After giving it another couple hard tugs, it finally came down with a loud bang and a huge cloud of dust.

Margaret and Liz coughed and pulled their shirts up over their nose and mouths while waving the dust away. Dave shook out his hat and dusted his clothes before placing his hat backwards on his head. Making his way up the creaky ladder, what he'd failed to see initially was revealed plainly—the opening of the attic at the top of the ladder was boarded shut.

"Well, this is very peculiar. Why would anyone board up

the entrance to the attic?" Dave pondered, pressing his hand into the board to try and move it.

Margaret and Liz stared up in astonishment.

"Your guess is as good as mine," Liz said with a shrug.

Dave grabbed the hammer and pry bar out of his tool belt he was wearing. "I'll try and remove these boards."

After five minutes of prying, Dave removed the boards and hoisted himself through the opening. When he finally got all the way into the attic, there was silence and just his footsteps. Margaret and Liz just looked at each other in anticipation.

Finally, Dave said, "I think you two need to see this. Get up here if you can."

Margaret and Liz eagerly made their way up the ladder, one after the other. Their jaws dropped once they got up there.

The attic had been transformed into a charming dormer bedroom. The walls were a bright green with colorful, hand-painted murals of flowers all over them. There were beautiful old hardwood floors, and a small window that looked out towards the ocean. In the corner sat a twin bed with a floral quilt on top, dust and cobwebs caked everything.

Margaret couldn't believe her eyes. "This is incredible. But why is this room boarded up and hidden away?"

Liz walked over to a small old door on the side of the room and studied it. "Hey, give me that skeleton key, I want to see something."

Margaret handed her the key, and Liz placed it into the keyhole and turned. The door opened.

When Liz saw what was behind the door, she was shocked.

"This is crazy. There's some small stairs. Where do they go? I feel like this is something you only see in the movies." Liz said with excitement.

"Here, I'll walk down to make sure they're safe," Dave said.

He had to duck through the small doorframe to get down the dark steps and use his cell phone flashlight to see where he was going. They heard his footsteps down the steps for what felt like an eternity.

"Do you see where they lead to?" Margaret bellowed down the steps.

"There's a door, but I can't get it to budge. It's either stuck or locked. Why don't one of you go downstairs and try to figure out where the opening is by my voice?"

Liz rushed out of the attic and downstairs to find this secret door. This was all too exciting, like they were on a treasure hunt.

"OK, keep talking so I can hear you," Liz said as she walked around the downstairs.

Dave made lots of noises, but they were so muffled. It was hard for Liz to figure out where they were coming from.

"Hey, Margaret. I think I need your help down here," Liz yelled up the stairs.

Margaret came down and waited to hear Dave.

"Hey, Dave, maybe bang on the wall or doorway. Your voice is too muffled," Margaret said as she walked the downstairs.

A moment later, a couple loud bangs came from the closet in the hallway. Margaret and Liz rushed over to the closet and opened it. It was just an old closest. They didn't see a doorway.

"Dave, make some more noise please," Margaret said while studying the inside of the closet.

This time, Dave sounded like he was right on the other side of the closet.

"Can you hear us, Dave?" Liz hollered into the closet.

"Yep. I think you're on the other side of the door. What does it look like on your end?"

"Well, it's the hallway closet. There's just a wall here inside of it. I don't see a doorway," Margaret said.

"Wait, what's that?" Liz shone her phone's flashlight on an indent in the wall that looked like the type of pull often found on sliding closet doors. Liz tugged on it. Nothing.

"Here, let me try. Just hold the flashlight there so I can see," Margaret said. She tugged as hard as she could and the painted wall board slid to the right three feet revealing Dave standing there covered in cobwebs and dust.

"Well, well, well. What have we here? A secret room, a hidden stairway, and now a concealed door obscured inside a closet. Boy, it sure seems someone was really trying to keep people from all of this," Dave said as he walked out of the closet, dusting himself off.

"This is seriously the most exciting thing ever. I love old houses." Margaret said while clapping her hands.

"We need to find the guest books, still. I'm going to head back up the stairs to see if they're up there," Liz said as she made her way back up the dark steps in the closet.

"Well, wait for me. I'm not missing out on any of this excitement," Margaret said, following close behind.

"Ladies, I'm going to get back to work in the basement for now to finish up. Let me know what else you find," Dave said as he made his way towards the basement.

"Will do. Thank you for your help, Dave," Margaret shouted back from up in the attic.

Liz and Margaret searched under the bed and in the little nooks for anything that resembled a guest book.

Margaret sighed and leaned against the wall in exhaustion. "I'm not seeing anything."

Liz decided to get on her hands and knees and look under the bed again. "Wait, I see something. It looks like a little crawl space door under the bed. It's painted the same as the wall so it blends in pretty well, but it's there alright." Liz stood back up on her feet.

"Here, let's move the bed out of the way so we can get a better look." Margaret grabbed one side of the bed since Liz had already grasped the other.

Having moved the bed, the crawl space door was clearly accessible, so Margaret got on her knees, yanked it open, and ducked down to look inside. It was a small space that had been part of the unfinished attic, but what she saw next blew her mind.

"Well, I think we found what we were looking for. It's stuffed to the brim with items. Here're the guest books. It looks like they had *a ton* of guests by how full they are," Margaret said as she placed them next to Liz and sat down beside her sister on the floor.

Liz blew the dust off the guest books and looked through them. "Wow, this one has a date from only ten years ago. I'm sure a lot of these guests are still around and would hopefully love to stay here again."

Margaret pulled out some more books. "Look at these! They made recipe books of what they cooked for guests. They must have given them away or sold them—there are ten copies here."

Liz dusted off the recipe books and looked through them. "Oh, we are definitely going to have to try these recipes out. I feel like this B&B just came to life from all of this, like we just discovered where its hidden secrets and magic rested."

Margaret smiled and peered back into the crawl space. "Well, I think that's it. I don't see anything—wait, what's that? I see some boxes. I'd probably need to get at least half of my body in there to reach them. Hold on …"

A few minutes later, Margaret had slid out eight boxes that had somehow fit in the tiny space. Opening them up revealed the most beautiful vintage Christmas decorations they had ever seen.

"These are antiques. They are absolutely gorgeous. Look at these glass ornaments."

"This is so exciting, but why is everything boarded up and hidden? I guess I'm not really understanding that part," Margaret said while admiring the items.

"I guess that's something we may or may not find out with

time," Liz said as she held up the most dazzling gold star Christmas tree topper.

They ferried everything down the secret stairway since it was safer and easier than using the attic ladder. They called for Dave down in the basement to see their treasures, and placed all of the books and boxes on and around the kitchen table. Everything was still pretty dusty, but they were too excited to care—they couldn't wait to look everything over.

CHAPTER FIVE

A couple days later, Margaret was suspicious again. Liz had been down in the basement almost the entire day with Dave and Greg, and they were all very vague about what they were doing. She heard hammering and things being moved for hours, and they were in and out of the basement door that opened into the backyard constantly. Whenever she would call down the steps to them about something, one of them would rush upstairs before she had a chance to even get in the basement.

"What is all that racket down there, and why do the stairs have red carpet on them now?" Margaret called from the top of the steps.

"Oh, um …Dave thinks the washer and dryer need to be fixed and moved to a better side of the basement. We are helping him. The carpet …is to … um … make it easier to walk down the steps," Liz said from somewhere in the basement.

"And that takes an entire day?"

"Maybe? I don't know."

Margaret could tell they were hiding something. *Doesn't this house have enough secrets already?*

Margaret had been on her laptop most of the day putting together fundraising for the Pinetree Wildlife Refuge or cooking up lunch and snacks for the secretive basement workers. By 3 p.m., it was time to pick up her girls and Liz and Greg's boys at school, and by dinnertime, Margaret had cooked a pot roast with potatoes and carrots and put together a side salad for everyone. The kids helped her set the table and fill the water glasses.

"OK, you guys. Dinner is ready," Margaret said down the basement steps. It had been awfully quiet in the basement the last hour or two.

Dave, Liz, and Greg appeared at the top of the stairs sweaty and dirty but with pure happiness on their faces. They fell into chairs at the table ready to devour their plates of food.

Margaret eyed them all up and laughed. "OK, when can I see this washer and dryer rearrangement?"

Dave took a bite of the pot roast and a long gulp of his iced tea. "I think after dinner is a good time."

Liz and Greg looked at each other with huge smiles on their faces.

"Just let me do a few more things down there after dinner, and we can show you what we did." Liz worked rather hard to subdue her excitement, but her sister knew that look anywhere.

After dinner, Margaret put her Nantucket cranberry pie on the table, hot out of the oven. It had been baking while they ate dinner, and she served everyone a hot cup of coffee or tea and placed some ice cream with a scooper next to the pie.

Dave took a bite of the hot cranberry pie with cold vanilla ice cream and savored every second it was in his mouth. The hot, crunchy crust of the pie and the soft coldness of the ice cream together made for the most wonderful texture and taste. He finished it with a gulp of his hot coffee, which he needed since he still planned on working through the night at the B&B.

"This is exquisite. Thank you so much, Margaret," Dave said as he took her hand in his across the table.

Margaret blushed and her heart warmed. "I'm so glad. I'm so grateful for all of your help. I'm not sure we could have taken on this B&B without you."

Liz cleared the table and loaded all the dishes to the dishwasher, then she grabbed Greg. "We'll be right back. Just have to do a couple things," she said as they hurried back down into the basement.

Dave laughed and shrugged at the confusion on Margaret's face. "I'm not saying a word. You'll see soon enough what all that racket was."

The kids had been in the living room playing games when Abby overheard Dave. "See what? I want to see."

Dave threw his arm around Abby as she tugged on his shirt, drawing her close, and gave her a soft noogie on her head while she screamed with laughter. "You guys will see shortly, dear Abby!"

Twenty minutes later Greg and Liz called from the basement for Margaret to come down. Margaret walked down the newly carpeted red steps into the somewhat dark basement. Dave and the kids followed behind her.

Once in the basement, it looked like a whole separate world from the rest of the house. It had been finished to look like an old retro drive-in theater and home movie theater in one. The basement was dimly lit with red carpet all around the room and thick red drapes that went all the way down to the floor on the two small windows. The ceiling was painted black with soft white string lights hung high on it to look like a starry night sky. Nailed up on the wall was an enormous canvas that Dave had painted of an old Chevy pickup truck at a drive-in theater with pillows in its bed. In the corner of the room, a vintage popcorn machine and a little table with a nice spread of candy that you'd find at the theater stood at the ready. There was a large flat screen TV with couches and recliners set up facing it, enough seating for probably a dozen people. On the walls, framed posters of some old movies and movie stars completed the look.

Margaret walked around the room studying everything they'd done. "This is unbelievable, guys! *This* is what you all have been doing down here? It's incredible. Movie nights will be a lot more exciting around here."

Liz, Greg and Dave high fived. Their plan had come together flawlessly, and they even got to surprise Margaret, which they had known would be no easy feat.

Margaret looked up at the ceiling. "Wow, you put in a drop ceiling with recessed lighting too."

"Yep, my friends helped me do that a while back. I even added some surround sound speakers in there," Dave said proudly.

The kids were excited beyond belief, jumping onto the recliners in the name of testing them out. "This is so cool! Our own home movie theater!" Liz and Greg's son Steven said.

"Wasn't this expensive? Do we have the permits to do this?" Margaret asked a little worried.

"Greg and I got the permit from the county after Dave told us his idea. We followed all the codes. Dave and his friends did this for free, and we brought the couches and TV in from Mom and Dad's storage unit. They offered since it's all been sitting for a few years. Greg and I purchased the recliners and the popcorn machine. I had a client give me a huge bonus, and I put some it towards this," Liz said feeling proud of herself.

"I still want to finish fixing up that side of the basement. I built a wall to section off the washer and dryer over there so you don't see all that," Dave said as he pointed to the far back side of the room.

"Will it get cold down here?" Margaret asked as she plopped on one of the couches next to Liz.

"Well, installing a new heating system was way too pricey, so the carpet will help and the insulation we added will help a ton. I'm going to add some top-of-the-line space heaters, and well, we'll just have to get cozy with some blankets, sweaters, and hot cocoa if needed," Dave said with a smile.

Margaret laid her head on her sister's shoulder as they sat on the couch, and all of the kids piled on top of them, laughing.

"We want to watch Christmas movies down here, Mom!" Harper said.

Margaret grabbed Harper and put her arm around her. "Oh, we definitely will do that, Harp. Now that you mention it, I think we should add a Christmas tree in that corner over there. We can make it movie theater themed. Did you kids want to help put that together this week?"

The kids couldn't agree fast enough. They were more than thrilled to do some more fun Christmas activities.

"Well, we need to be getting home. The boys need to do their homework and get ready for bed," Liz said yawning.

Michael and Steven silently protested, crossing their arms and not budging from their recliners.

"Boys, I'm not kidding. Hop to it. Grab your stuff upstairs," Liz said sternly.

Margaret yawned. "Yeah, I think we're going to follow your lead. The girls also need to get their reading done."

Dave looked back towards the washer and dryer. "I'm off tomorrow, so is it cool if I stay late tonight to try and finish up the other side of the basement? I'll lock up before I leave."

"Of course, Dave. Whatever you're comfortable with. Just let me know if you need anything." Margaret gave him a big hug goodbye, and the girls encircled his legs and waist with a big hug of their own at the same time.

* * *

At 9 p.m. Dave heard a knock at the front door. A little confused by who would be knocking at this hour, he hesitated answering it until he peeked through the side window and saw a man. When he opened the door, he immediately recognized Paul.

Paul look disappointed to see Dave. "Oh, hi. Is Margaret here? The girls said that they'd be here today."

Dave crossed his arms and leaned his shoulder into the door frame. "Nope, they all left a couple hours ago. Can I help you with something?"

Paul squinted his eyes. "You must be Dave."

Dave held his hand out. "Yep, that's me. And you're Paul?"

Paul just looked at his hand. "Yes."

Dave pulled his hand back and put it in his pocket. "Well, maybe you can give her a call since they're not here."

"I guess so," Paul said as he stood staring at the ground, sad and defeated.

"Look, man. I have a few things to finish inside so I need to be heading back in. Just give her a call."

"Wait," Paul said abruptly as Dave started to close the door.

Dave sighed. "Listen, Paul, I understand you and Margaret got a divorce, but I'm not sure I'm the person to be discussing these matters with right now."

"That's not what I want to talk about."

Dave motioned for Paul to come in, throwing the door open wide. "Take a seat in the kitchen. I've got some hot tea going if you want any."

Paul took a seat and clasped his hands together. Dave brought over two mugs of tea.

"Sandy and I had a fight. That's who I am dating—rather, engaged to," Paul said while taking a long gulp of hot tea.

"Oh, I know Sandy. She's best friends with my ex-wife," Dave said matter-of-factly.

Paul look confused. "Wait. So, you're telling me that Michelle is your ex-wife? How did I not know this?"

Dave shrugged. "Beats me. We did all run into each other that one time at the Washington Street Mall, and it was super awkward. They never said anything to you about who I was? I'm surprised."

Paul sighed. "Nope. I'm finding Sandy lies and keeps a lot of secrets. I'm just now learning she's been engaged four times over the past ten years. I'm not sure what else she's been hiding."

Dave chuckled sympathetically. "Wow, even I know she's been engaged four times in only ten years. She leaves right when they start wedding planning and moves on to the next guy. That woman seems meant to be a free bird."

Paul looked embarrassed and dropped his head into his hands. "Oh, what have I done? I ruined my marriage for this woman. I'm beyond stupid."

Dave didn't say anything.

Paul looked over at Dave. "What happened for you and Michelle to get divorced anyway?"

Dave took a long gulp of tea, set his mug down and paused. "Well, Will was my best friend and Michelle was my wife of ten years. I caught them cheating and ended the friendship and divorced Michelle."

Paul just shook his head in disbelief. "That is awful, and I'm so sorry. Then again, I cheated on Margaret. I'm no better."

Dave shrugged. He wanted to agree, but didn't want to kick someone while they were down.

Paul stared at his hands. "Margaret mentioned to me that my mother told her she didn't like Sandy and that she thought she was controlling me. It made me mad when I heard that, but I took time to think about it, and realized she *has* been passively controlling how often I see my girls and my parents. Boy, if she knew I were here right now, she would flip out."

Dave shook his head. "I don't think it's my place to give you advice here, but you really need to consider everything before you go through with that marriage. A good person would never keep you from the people you love."

Paul leaned back in his chair and looked around. "Wow, this place is stunning. Have you been working on it a lot?"

Dave got up to put the empty mugs in the dishwasher. "Yep, I have. I love being here. My buddies have been helping me out too. Want to see what I'm finishing up in the basement?"

Paul stood from the table with a little more happiness in his eyes. "Yeah, that sounds great."

Paul followed Dave into the basement and was blown away by the home drive-in movie theater. "OK, wait. You made all of this? This was completely unfinished prior?"

Dave turned the TV on, dimmed the recess lighting, turned on the star string light ceiling, and turned up the sound system. "Yep, and check this out."

Within moments, a thriller movie came on with surround sound from all directions of the room. That, paired with the starry night ceiling made for the most unique and fun viewing experience.

Paul plopped into a recliner and laid back. "This is crazy awesome. You've got some skills."

Dave took a load off in the recliner next to him, admiring his work. "Thank you, I try. What is your thing? What do you do?"

Paul immediately piped up, happy to talk about something he loves. "I'm a musician. That's my thing. I love playing, making, and listening to music."

"That's great. I never learned to play an instrument. Always wanted to. What style of music do you play?"

"Oh, all kinds. Rock, country, classical—you name it. But jazz is my favorite."

"Very cool. Maybe you can play for the guests here someday."

Paul laughed. "Maybe? I don't know if Margaret would want that."

Dave chuckled, shrugging his shoulders. He'd give him

that. Maybe Margaret wouldn't go that far in the name of harmony. But maybe she would, she was extraordinary like that.

Paul looked over at Dave. "You know, I'm kind of jealous of what you and Margaret have. You're a good guy, and I can tell you're good to her and the girls. The girls love you, which made me a little uncomfortable at first, but now I appreciate it. They need as many people to love them as possible. I only wish I had the same kind of relationship right now."

Dave nodded, not sure what to say to that.

Paul went on. "You know what the fight was about with Sandy today? I told her I'm going to visit my mother on Sundays again, and I'm not canceling on the girls anymore unless something super important came up. I didn't ask her. I told her. She got mad. She literally got *mad* at that. She feels that all time should be spent with her and nobody else, unless she approves. I stormed out of the house and came to talk to Margaret. I don't have anyone else to talk to right now that knows my situation. I know—awkward, right?"

Dave sighed, feeling bad for him. "I get it, man. You've got a lot of thinking to do. It sounds like you're making some better decisions for yourself and your girls though. Keep at it."

Paul looked over at Dave. "It was great talking to you. I'm glad I stopped by. I really needed this. I've never had many guy friends. I guess I kind of keep to myself. Margaret always pushed me to play at open mic nights and to meet other musicians, but I was always lazy and shy about it. Margaret is the exact opposite of Sandy. Even though Margaret and my mother didn't get along very well, she always made sure I visited my parents regularly and invited them over every so often for visits."

Dave stood from his recliner, ready to call it a night. He switched everything off in the room. "Anytime, my man."

Paul extended his hand to Dave. "Let's do this right this time," he said with a smile.

Dave shook his hand and reached his arm around Paul's back for a big man-hug-back-slap.

"So, we'll see you soon? You'll have to get the grand tour of this place next time," Dave said as they headed towards the front door.

Paul walked out onto the porch then turned back. "I don't get it. You don't seem like you hate me or anything. Why is that? I'm the cheating ex-husband of your girlfriend. I'm no better than Will."

Dave thought for a moment. "Well, all things led to this," he said while looking around the B&B. "If the past was different, I wouldn't be dating Margaret or working on this marvelous old B&B or have the girls or the rest of Margaret's great family in my life. I'm the happiest I've ever been. I simply don't have any room or desire for hate or jealousy."

CHAPTER SIX

Margaret and Liz met at the B&B the next day prepared to get to work. It was a rainy, overcast, chilly morning. You could hear the pitter-patter of rain all around the Seahorse. They made some hot coffee and sat at the kitchen table with their laptops and supplies. They needed to bring business to the B&B and were ready to go through the guest books.

"Wow, I can't believe how many guests are in here," Liz said as she flipped through the dusty pages.

Margaret grabbed a book, opening to the first page. "This one starts in the 1980s. Should I even contact guests from this far back? They only have mailing addresses, and who knows if they even still live there?

Liz thought for a moment. "It can't hurt. I say we mail out postcards and send e-mails to everyone who listed them."

"I bought a ton of stamps and had these beautiful post-cards made with photos of the B&B and the contact information," Margaret said, grabbing a huge stack out of her bag.

"Fabulous! Well, let's get to work addressing these post-cards and sending out e-mails. There are thousands of names here," Liz said as she put a handful of pens on the kitchen table.

They both sighed knowing how much work was ahead of them to bring the B&B back to life.

"Hi, ladies," Sarah said as she came through the door and took off her raincoat, hanging it on the coat rack by the door.

"Hey, Sarah. We're in here," Margaret called from the kitchen.

Sarah walked in looking like a drenched rat. She immediately grabbed a hot cup of coffee, sat across from them at the kitchen table, and threw her hair up in a bun like she meant business.

"I'm here to help. I know I've been a little MIA lately, but I'm excited about this B&B and ready to dig in with whatever you two need."

Liz smiled and sighed. "You couldn't have come at a better time. We have thousands of these postcards to address and e-mails to send. if you'd like to grab a guest book and start from the first page that would help us immensely."

Margaret laughed. "I hope you have all day to spend on this. This is literally going to take hours to do."

Sarah sighed. "Yeah, I have all the time in the world these days. My contract with my job didn't get renewed several months ago. I've been feeling pretty down lately."

"Oh, no. Your school counselor job? You love that job and your students. Why were you laid off?" Liz asked.

Sarah copied addresses onto the postcards while talking. "Well, it had to do with budgets. The other school counselors have been there forever, so I was the lowest on the ladder. Some other departments in the school had layoffs too. It's not an ideal situation. I haven't talked about it much to anyone really. I thought I'd find another job with my experience, but it just hasn't worked out yet."

"I'm so sorry, Sarah. However, I think you'll get through this stronger and better." Margaret could always be counted on to stay optimistic.

"That's awful, Sarah. I'm sorry to hear this. What about

Mark? The guy we met recently? Are you two still seeing each other?" Liz asked.

Sarah sighed again. "Well, yes and no. Right after you guys met him, he had to go abroad for a work trip. He might be there past Christmas. It's all up in the air. We talk every day, but it's just super confusing right now."

Margaret cleared her throat. "Well, you're here with us now in this beautiful old B&B, and we're going to have fun today while we work. It will keep your mind off things for a while."

Sarah smiled. "Thanks, guys."

Liz grabbed her laptop and started typing. "I have an idea. How about you two work on the post cards and e-mails, and I can see about running some ads about the reopening in the local paper. I can also update the website and social media page. I was thinking we could create some fun events to bring some attention to the Seahorse while making a little profit."

"I'm liking this idea, sister."

"Now to think of what kind of events we could do ..."

"Oh, I know something perfect," Sarah said, grabbing her phone and looking something up.

Sarah showed her phone to Liz. "This is my friend's ceramic painting business. She has a studio in Cape May where you can go and paint ceramics. I bet she may be willing to set something up here for you, though she would have to take everything back to the studio to be fired and finished in the kiln."

Margaret squealed and clasped her hands together. "I've always wanted to paint those old ceramic Christmas trees with the lights. You know, like the one Mom painted eons ago that she still puts out every Christmas?"

Liz smiled. "Yes. I've been looking for a vintage one at thrift shops for myself, and they are so hard to find. I really want a white one with blue lights."

Sarah laughed. "Give my friend a call and ask. Tell her you know me."

A few hours later, hundreds of post cards and e-mails had been addressed and sent, respectively. Liz had called Sarah's friend and arranged for a catered event in two weeks at the B&B for ceramic Christmas tree painting. Additionally, she'd created a bunch more events for December, and placed them on the social media page.

"OK, this is what I've come up with for December's event ideas. The ceramic night is already booked. If we can't fill it with guests, we'll just invite our family and friends over to make up for it, but I think it may just work. So, here's my list."

1. Hot cocoa firepit nights with Christmas song sing-alongs

2. Old Christmas movie nights in basement and/or living room

3. Breakfast with Santa

4. Christmas tree ceramic painting

"This is great, Liz. I love all of these ideas," Sarah said enthusiastically.

"I'm loving this too, but I'm starving. I'm going to start getting lunch together for us. I can't believe it's already noon. We've been at this for a while now," Margaret said as she got up and made her to way to the fridge.

"Yes, I'm famished," Liz said.

"Well, since it's a rainy day, how about I make us some grilled cheese with apples, and I can warm up the leftover tomato soup I made the other day," Margaret said as she pulled items out of the fridge.

"Oh, I love apples in my grilled cheese sandwich. The sweetness paired with the saltiness of the cheese is divine," Sarah said.

"Perfect! I'll get to it!" Margaret said as she preheated a pan.

Moments later, Dave walked in soaking wet. He hadn't worn a raincoat like Sarah.

"Well, if it's not the most beautiful women in Cape May."

The three most beautiful women in Cape May laughed, and Liz said, "You're too kind, Dave," with pink flooding her cheeks.

Crossing the room to where Margaret stood at the stove, he enveloped her from behind, wrapping her in a big hug while nestling his face into the crook of her neck. "Hello, my darling. What are you cooking?"

Margaret's whole body turned to Jell-O. He knew exactly how to elicit butterflies in her stomach these days. Then again, she may have told him at one point that hugs from behind did that to her. They made her feel protected and loved at the same time. Something Paul never did for her.

"I'm making us grilled cheese with apples and tomato soup. Would you like some?"

"Oh, I'd love some. After I'm done, I thought I'd go inspect that secret bedroom in the attic to see if it's OK to be used," Dave said while pouring a cup of coffee.

"Secret bedroom in the attic? Am I hearing this correctly?" Sarah asked as her eyes sparkled with curiosity.

Margaret threw the pot of tomato soup on the stove to warm and looked over at Liz. "We never told her about the attic bedroom."

Sarah shot up out of her chair. "I need to see this bedroom. Pronto. I can't believe I'm just now hearing about this. You both know I'm super into this stuff."

Dave laughed. "I'll show you after lunch since I'm heading up there anyway."

Sarah sat back down with anxious excitement. "This day just got a whole lot better between the grilled cheese and the secret attic bedroom."

Margaret and Liz laughed. "We'll all go up together. It will be a nice break from all this work," Margaret said.

After a scrumptious lunch, they ushered Sarah to the hallway closet.

"The stairs are in *the closet?* This just gets better and better,"

Sarah said as she eagerly followed them up.

"We need to add a light for this stairwell. It's way too dark," Liz said, feeling her away around as she climbed the stairs.

"I was going to look into that, among some other things," Dave said.

They opened the door to the attic room, and it looked more beautiful than before, but still very dusty.

"We still have to clean this room and figure out what we're going to do with it," Margaret said as she wiped her finger down the wall and looked at the dust now caked on it.

"Agreed. It will have to come after we get all these post-cards and e-mails sent out, though. All of that takes priority," Liz said as she took a pillow off the bed and whacked it, causing a cloud of dust to float from the fabric.

Dave walked around the room, quietly eyeing it up and down.

Margaret sighed. "What are you thinking, Dave? Is this room usable? It only seems to fit a twin bed. I'm not sure how many guests will want to stay at a B&B alone, and even if they came alone, wouldn't they want a nice big queen or king bed instead of a twin?"

"Well, the electric needs a little tweaking as the light up here keeps flickering. It does have some heat running to it, which is a bonus. The hatch door needs something around it so nobody tries to use it and hurt themselves. Everyone really should only use the stairs to come up here unless it's one of us. There isn't a private bath, so whoever stays in this room would have to use the common bathroom downstairs. Not sure how convenient or desirable that would be …"

Liz walked over to a book shelf in the corner that held old dusty novels. Opening one, she flipped through the pages. "This room wouldn't be very inviting, and we wouldn't be able to charge much for it. I'm not sure it's a very suitable guest room."

Margaret slunk down into a sitting position on the floor. "You're probably right. I guess we could just use this room for storage."

Sarah looked out the window towards the ocean. Just then, a horse-drawn carriage went by and some passersby, bundled up in sweaters and hats, walked by with their to-go hot drink cups. They stopped and marveled at the Seahorse, then took photos of it and continued on.

"I've got it!" Sarah said as she turned away from the window. "Why don't you make this room magically decorated for Christmas and sign the house up for the Cape May Candle-light Christmas Tour, and advertise the secret attic room as the pièce de résistance. People love that kind of stuff. They eat it up. While the room probably isn't best for being used by guests, it very well may drum up *a lot* of attention and business because of how fascinating it is. Maybe even offer your own tour at some point so you can continue with them after Christmas. Also, my friend writes for the local paper. She would probably love to do a story on the Seahorse and the secret attic bedroom. Actually, let me text her now."

Margaret and Liz squealed in excitement. "You're brilliant, Sarah," Margaret said while giving her a huge hug.

Dave laughed. "Well, I have to say, I like that idea. It definitely gives this old B&B a lot more character and mystery."

Liz thought for a moment. "Last I checked, they already had all the houses and B&Bs scheduled for the tour. They probably schedule out months in advance. Not sure if we'll be able to squeeze in."

"It can't hurt to try," Sarah said optimistically.

Margaret studied the room and bit her lip. "Maybe we can use some of those antique Christmas decorations we found in the crawl space. I think I saw a vintage white Christmas tree in one of the larger boxes. That would look perfect up here. We still have to go through all of those treasures."

Sarah shrieked, "OK, my friend just texted me back and

said she would love to write a piece about the B&B. She has actually been searching for a nice feel-good piece to add into *this weekend's paper*. She asked if she can stop by later today? They go to press tomorrow for Saturday morning publication. It's a small local paper but it's also online, and they have a huge amount of loyal readers."

"Perfect. Tell her that works, and I'll tell Greg that I'll be home late. I'm going downstairs to get to work on trying to get the B&B in the candlelight tour. This just may be one of the most productive days ever," Liz said she hurried down the steps towards the kitchen.

Sarah followed Liz down the steps, and it was just Margaret and Dave in the attic.

Dave leaned his shoulder against the wall and looked over at Margaret. "So, while I have you here, I figure I'll tell you what happened last night when I stayed late to work."

Margaret looked surprised. "What do you mean?"

Dave chuckled. "Well, it's a funny story, actually. Paul came by looking for you around nine—"

"What?! Why on earth would he do that?"

Dave continued on. "Well, he was surprised to catch me here and didn't seem very happy about it at first. But he was desperate to talk to someone, so I invited him inside. He told me he had a fight with Sandy. She didn't approve of him standing up to her about how controlling she was. He found out she's been lying to him and keeping secrets. He seems to understand that he's not in a good relationship. I'm pretty sure he's probably going to break it off if he hasn't already. I ended up showing him the basement, and we kind of bonded. It was strange but nice at the same time."

Margaret was silent for a moment before looking over at Dave with tears in eyes.

Dave immediately moved across the room and wrapped his arms around her, kissing her forehead. "Are you OK?"

Margaret wiped her eyes with her sleeve. "Oh, I'm

perfectly fine. I'm just dating the most perfect man in existence is all." Dave smiled and hugged Margaret tighter. "I had a similar talk with him, but I think he really just needed to hear it from another man. He doesn't really have any male friends in his life to do that with, so thank you. I hate to see my daughters' father with someone who doesn't care anything about them or spending time with them. It's heartbreaking. Well, I'd better get back downstairs and continue on with the postcards and e-mails."

Dave nodded. "I think I'm going to hang up here and see what I can work on today."

Margaret made her way back to Sarah and Liz in the kitchen, a room which now crackled with excitement.

"What are you two so happy about?'

"Well, we are officially booked for the Cape May Candlelight Christmas Tour. It starts this weekend, so we'd better get moving. We have two days!" Liz doing a happy dance made Margaret smile.

"My friend said she'll be here around dinnertime for the interview," Sarah said as she happily addressed postcards.

"I have an idea. How about I'll go clean the attic bedroom up and get it ready for decorating. Then we can decorate it tomorrow and get it all ready for the tour. You two can stay down here and continue on with the e-mails and postcards. I'll have Greg pick up all the kids after school, and they'll stay with him at our house," Liz said as she made her way to the closet to grab cleaning supplies.

"Perfect. Since we'll be here late, I'll throw something quick in the oven for dinner," Margaret said as she sat down at the kitchen table, ready to get back to work on the postcards.

Liz stood by the closet with all of the cleaning supplies in her hands and looked over at Margaret and Sarah with a smile on her face. "It's amazing how this all came together so quickly. I really think it's going to work out."

CHAPTER SEVEN

The next day, family and friends were invited over for a dinner that was more or less tantamount to bribery for more help decorating the B&B. Margaret and Liz went out in the morning and found some great movie-themed ornaments at a local shop for the basement Christmas tree that the kids were decorating.

The attic was all cleaned up and ready for some Christmas spirit, so Margaret, Liz, Judy, Sarah, and couple of their aunts sat on the floor, digging into boxes of old-timey decorations to see what treasures they could find.

Margaret first went to the box where she'd seen the white Christmas tree, except it wasn't white after all. It was a seven-foot silver aluminum tree.

Judy and the aunts gasped as Margaret assembled the tree in the corner of the attic. "We had that exact tree in the 1960s. I have such fond memories of us decorating it with blue ball ornaments and putting gobs of tinsel all over it," Judy said with a smile.

Aunt Linda agreed. "Yes, we had one too. They were very popular back then. They were lit by a color wheel on the bottom that rotated different colors onto the tree. It was so magical."

"Is this the color wheel?" Liz asked as she pulled something that matched that description out of the box.

"That's it! Wow, this is quite special," Aunt Linda said as she took it from Liz to study it.

Margaret smiled as she put together the tree and fluffed it up.

Liz laughed. "Well, would you look at this! I guess they also decorated this tree with blue ball ornaments and tinsel. There is a ton in this box."

"Oh, my! I feel like a kid again. Let's get this tree decorated properly, ladies," Aunt Debbie said as she walked over to the tree, ornaments in hand.

Sarah turned on an up-tempo 1950s Christmas song playlist from her phone, and the room got even livelier and joyful seconds later. The aunts and Judy danced while decorating, meanwhile Liz, Margaret, and Sarah continued to sift through the boxes while bobbing along. It felt like a mini Christmas party in the tiny attic bedroom.

Liz placed some battery-operated candles around the room and down the steps while Sarah and Margaret found some vintage Santas and other items to place around the room.

Moments later, Dave and Greg popped their heads in and laughed.

"What in the world is going on up here?" Greg smiled.

The ladies kept dancing. Judy looked over at Dave and grabbed his hand for a twirl. "Come on, Dave! Join our secret attic Christmas party!"

Liz looked over at Greg and laughed and shrugged. "They're really into it, if you couldn't tell."

Bob, who had been watching movies in the basement with some of the uncles while the kids decorated, also popped his head in the room because of all of the noise.

Judy smiled while twirling with Aunt Debbie to the music

and immediately ran over to Bob for a dance. Bob was ready because he grabbed her, spun her around, and dipped her. Judy had made him take dance lessons with her for years and it showed.

"Did you guys want to join in on the fun?" Margaret half joked.

Greg laughed. "Well, Dave and I thought we could all go out and pick a live Christmas tree for the foyer after dinner. Not that any of you are lacking Christmas spirit today, but a local farm has hayrides to the trees, which will be a lot of fun. Just an idea."

"Oh, I'm loving this idea. Are you talking about the Brewer's Tree Farm? It's so beautifully lit at night, and they have a fire pit with s'mores and hot cider and cocoa afterwards. I say we do it. What do you all think?" Liz asked excitedly.

"Well, how about you all go," Judy said to the younger crowd, "and we'll stay back and finish decorating the attic and get dinner going." The aunts nodded enthusiastically. "Your father and uncles can get a fire going in the living room. Just don't let the kids lose their appetites with those s'mores," Judy laughed.

"Perfect. Let's go get the kids bundled up. Maybe we can bring some blankets to put over our laps on the hayride," Margaret said as she made her way down the steps with the guys.

"Mom, here's a box of recipes books and other things. Maybe you can find something in here for dinner. We haven't had time to go through them yet," Liz said.

"Oh, lovely. I bet some of the recipes were adored by guests. We'll see what we can find," Aunt Linda said as she grabbed a book and flipped through a few pages.

Fifteen minutes later, and they were all bundled up and out the door to go to the Christmas tree farm hayride.

When they arrived, they immediately were led by one of Santa's elves to the line for the hayride since Dave had the foresight to purchase tickets online to save some waiting time. After a short wait, they finally got on the tractor-driven hayride which wound its way throughout the brightly decorated farm. The air was crisp and chilly, and the stars were beaming above. As they admired the Christmas lights display, a small old speaker full of crackling and static played Christmas tunes while the hayride weaved around different parts of the farm. Margaret and Dave cozied up under a blanket with Harper and Abby on either side of them. The same with Liz and Greg. Sarah sat alone with her own blanket looking happy for the most part, albeit she did a good job at hiding sadness in her eyes.

Margaret's heart sank a little knowing Mark was probably on her mind. "Come over here next to Abby, Sarah. It's much warmer."

Sarah smiled and made her way over to Abby, who immediately laid her head on Sarah's shoulder.

The hayride stopped abruptly, and another elf appeared to lead them all off and give instructions on how to pick a tree.

The kids took off running through the trees. Some bright edison-style string lights hung overhead and helped not only to see everything they had to offer but also to add to the already festive atmosphere.

"So, what are we thinking? We have a pretty high ceiling in the foyer. Do we want to go with something grand? A statement piece?" Margaret asked while gazing out at the hundreds of trees.

Liz clapped her heads. "Oh, yes. That's a great idea."

They all walked around for a while enjoying each other's company. They browsed the farm's various sections, each one growing a different type of Christmas tree. As Margaret perused the Douglas firs, she accidentally bumped into someone.

She whirled around to see their grouchy next-door neighbors.

"Oh, excuse me. I'm so sorry about that. I didn't see you there," Margaret said hurriedly before they noticed who she was. It was too late.

The woman had a scowl on her face. "Wait a minute. Are you the two women I see next door to us at The Seahorse Inn all of the time?"

The guys, Sarah, and the kids had all wandered off leaving just Liz and Margaret to face off with the neighbors.

"Yes, that's us. I don't believe we've been introduced," Liz said, holding out her hand.

The woman just looked at Liz's hand before looking back up at them. "You two are related to Henry and Barbara, I'm assuming?"

"Well, sort of. They are our great uncle's parents. We've only met them once or twice," Margaret said, feeling a little angry at how impolite this woman was.

The woman laughed. "Figures! Are those two dead yet? They must be as old as the dickens by now."

Margaret and Liz stood stock-still, shocked by the complete rudeness of this woman. They knew her name only because their friendly neighbor John had told them, but they weren't going to let her know that.

"No, they're alive and well. Living the dream, actually," Liz said, knowing full well that was a bit of lie. She didn't care. Who was this woman to ask if they were dead yet? Had she no heart?

The woman's husband laughed and walked away, leaving just his wife now. She squinted her eyes and glared at them. "Well, I don't know what your plans are with that B&B, but you *will not* be ruining everything we've worked hard for next door at our B&B. Is that clear?"

Margaret and Liz stared at her with blank expressions. Cape May was loaded with B&Bs. A lot of them being next door to each other. In fact, there was another B&B on the other side of those neighbors. They obviously all did pretty well since they had remained open all of these years. Why was this woman so bent out of shape about *their* bed-and-breakfast?

The woman didn't wait for an answer and walked away, throwing her hands up in the air.

"Are you *kidding* me? Is this real? Who does this lady think she is?" Liz growled out towards her.

Margaret threw her head back in annoyance. "Well, I have no idea what she is talking about. She obviously has issues. Let's not let this ruin our fun night, OK? It's been such a wonderful day otherwise. Let's take a quick walk to calm down before we go find everyone else."

After ten minutes, Margaret and Liz had blown off enough steam and agreed to not bring up their encounter to anyone else until later. They found everyone gathered around what appeared to be the perfect tree.

"Well, what do you think? She's about ten feet tall, and will fit perfectly in the foyer with those vaulted ceilings," Dave said while proudly eyeing the pristine Fraser fir.

"Oh, it's gorgeous!" Liz and Margaret both said.

They informed the employees, who tagged their tree and took care of the rest, then they hopped back on the hayride toward the cars. They were met at the end of the hayride by fire pits, a meet-and-greet with Santa, and some food stands set up with make-your-own-s'more kits, hot drinks, and other delectables.

Abby and Harper couldn't wait to see Santa while Liz and Greg's boys were old enough to know the truth about the man in the red suit. They opted for some s'mores by the fire instead.

They made their way back to the B&B with the tree tied down in the back of Dave's truck and arrived to the most delicious smells that filled the entire B&B.

Judy made her way out of the kitchen, wiping her hands on her apron. "Well, you came back just in time. The table is set and ready, and we cooked up a few things for dinner I think you all will like."

Aunt Debbie filled the few last glasses on the table with water. "We were going to use something from the B&B cookbook, but most of the recipes were for breakfast and brunch since that's what they served here. We did find one cookbook with lots of notes written in it, and it was fun to see what were guest favorites. You should really look that over for recipes to use."

"Everything smells amazing! Thanks for letting us know about the cookbook. We will surely add those recipes to our list," Liz said as she took a seat at the table.

"Take a look at this," Aunt Linda said as she handed the open cookbook to Liz.

"It's a blurb about the history of the Seahorse. People love to hear the stories of the old bed-and-breakfasts around here. You should read it. It's quite interesting."

Margaret walked behind Liz to read it too.

A Note From the Innkeeper:

The Seahorse Inn was built in 1879 after a fire destroyed it two years prior. It was bought by a wealthy man in Philadelphia who wanted a seaside vacation home for his large family. It was designed by the famous architect William James who was known for designing some of the most beautiful Victorian homes in Cape May.

It boasts nine bedrooms with the tenth bedroom added last minute in the attic for their nanny. This attic bedroom had a secret stairwell leading to it from the hallway closet, which is still there today. It was used as a vacation home and passed down from generation to generation until 1950 when it was bought by Frank and Gladys Smith and turned into a guest house, which they operated until 1970. They sold to the current owners, Henry and Barbara Lambert, who then restored much of the property and turned it into the successful bed-and-breakfast it is today.

"This is so neat. I'm glad we have some better historical knowledge. It all makes more sense now. We definitely need this for the house tour this month and for the website," Margaret said.

The fire crackled in the other room while the family sat

around the candlelit table eating, laughing, and telling stories. Aunt Debbie made her famous tortellini soup, and Aunt Linda made cheesy, crusty cornbread with a nice big salad full of vegetables, hardboiled eggs, and croutons. On the side was homemade blue cheese dressing. Judy made a pumpkin cheese-cake, which had just enough time to cool to be ready to eat after dinner. Being gathered together was something that made Margaret's heart flutter, especially when Dave was beside her looking happy as a clam.

After dessert and coffee, Dave and Greg lugged the tree in from the truck and set it up in the foyer while everyone watched. It looked even bigger once it was in the house, and the room immediately filled with the sharp, sweet aroma that was quintessentially Christmas. Some music could be heard from the kitchen, and an old holiday movie was playing in the living room for the kids.

Dave, Greg, and some uncles helped string the white lights around the tree and fluff it up, while Judy and the aunts went back to clean up the kitchen so they could be ready to decorate the tree by the time it was done being lit.

Margaret and Liz went up and grabbed the rest of the boxes from the attic, half of which hadn't even been opened yet, and brought them down to the foyer for everyone to decorate the tree with.

Margaret opened a box to find delicate blown glass orna-ments packaged safely in their original boxes.

"Wow. Look at all of this," Margaret said as she displayed a box of the ornaments to everyone in the room.

Judy and the aunts hurried back in the foyer to see.

"My oh my. Aren't those stunning? Those are quite a trea-sure, dear. Take good care of them," Aunt Linda said as she gently grabbed one to hang on the tree.

All too quickly, with the help of everyone there, the last ornament was placed on the tree and it was nearly complete.

The last thing left was the mercury glass tree topper, and Margaret did the honors.

Turning off all of the rooms' lights, the family marveled at the beauty of the tree. Aunts, uncles, and Judy and Bob put their arms around each other while Margaret and Dave and Liz and Greg did the same. Dave grabbed Sarah and put his other arm around her so she didn't feel left out.

"Hey, I'm going to go see what it looks like from outside through the window," Margaret said as she rushed out onto the sidewalk.

Dave followed closely behind. They got out to the sidewalk with the air so cold they could see their breath and the moon so bright it reflected off the ocean across the street. The house was lit magnificently both on the outside and now on the inside. The foyer tree could be seen perfectly from this vantage point.

"It's perfect. Everything is perfect," Margaret said while giving Dave a big hug.

"I'm pretty sure you're perfect too," Dave said with a smile.

Margaret squeezed him tighter. Then, something caught her eye over at the rude neighbors' B&B. It was the owners having a romantic moment standing with their arms wrapped each other looking out towards the ocean. They didn't seem to notice Margaret or Dave standing out front. It was the first time that Margaret had seen them look happy.

"Well, look over there. It's the neighbors who hate us," Margaret said, motioning to them with a head tilt.

Dave looked over at them and chuckled. "Well, I guess they aren't always angry."

Margaret laughed. "Oh, I didn't tell you what happened at the Christmas tree farm. We bumped into them, moreso the woman. She refused to shake Liz's hand and warned us to not ruin their bed-and-breakfast. She asked if my Uncle Lou's parents were dead yet. Can you believe the nerve of that lady?"

Dave shook his head and thought for a moment. "I'm

betting something much deeper went on between them that caused all of this. I'm sure all of it will come to light eventually."

Margaret walked towards the steps. "You're probably right. I'm not sure I even want to know at this point. It's not my battle to fight. It has nothing to do with us."

Dave chuckled. "I think the neighbors just made it your battle."

CHAPTER EIGHT

It was Saturday morning, and the candlelight tour was hours away. The article on the reopening of The Seahorse Inn and the secret attic room went out that morning in the papers and online. By now, most of the postcards they sent to former guests in the guest books had been delivered, and the social media page was getting a lot more interest due to the events Liz had organized and posted days prior. Being included in the Candlelight Christmas Tour last minute was just the icing on the cake.

Everything they'd done had worked. The phone rang off the hook, and they were getting tons of e-mails. Old guests and new guests alike were excited to book their stay at the Seahorse. Even some ghost hunters took interest in booking a stay there, which made Margaret and Liz giggle.

They sat at the kitchen table enjoying a relaxing cup of coffee while looking at their laptops before the exciting but busy day got away from them.

"Did you see this? There's close to seventy-five unread e-mails this morning. I've already responded to twenty-five, but the list keeps growing!" Liz said as she pointed to her screen.

"Well, we sure got what we wished for. The B&B is back, alive and well, it seems,"

Liz nodded and sighed. "I have to say, though, and I hate to be a downer, but I'm exhausted. We've been working night and day, and I can't even remember what my normal life before this was like. Greg and I even got in a fight the other night about me never being home anymore. He understands that it won't always be like this, but I think he's just a little frustrated and stressed, especially with the boys and getting them to all of their sports practices and other activities."

Margaret took a gulp of her coffee and set it down. "You're right. We can't continue on like this. It will burn us out. We have other jobs and our families. I've been bringing the girls over here so I'm still with them all of the time, but I definitely feel like we need to have more of our regular routines at home back. We're going to have to hire people to help make this work for us."

"Did someone say hire people to help?" Sarah walked into the kitchen, unraveling the large scarf around her neck.

"Yep. You wouldn't believe it. Our e-mails and phone are blowing up today with bookings since that article came out. Thank you so much for coordinating that with your friend," Liz said.

Margaret chimed in, "But now we're scrambling to start looking for help. We've realized that we're about to really get in over our heads."

Sarah clapped her hands and jumped up and down. "Hire me! I'm laid off, and I need a job. Plus, I was thinking of looking into a career change anyway. I'm still working on figuring out the details of that. I love counseling, but I'm pretty burnt out. However, I've always dreamed of working at a quaint B&B and getting to know all of the guests who come to stay. Plus, I'll have the ocean and beach *right here* at my fingertips."

Liz jumped up and hugged her. "Perfect! I'm loving this idea!"

Margaret laughed. "It'll be a hoot working together again like the good old days in high school at the pizza shop."

Sarah jabbed her finger into Margaret's side. "Except there won't be any marinara sauce flinging fights here. Remember that? It looked like a murder scene afterwards. I had to be hosed off just to be able to get in my parents' car. I smelled like tomatoes for days!"

They all laughed for what felt like five minutes straight.

Liz thought for a moment and turned to Margaret. "I have an idea. How about you and I work here a few days a week. That will give us enough time off for our other jobs and our families. We can hire a house cleaner and a couple people to work nights and a couple to work days when we're not here, and of course Sarah will be here."

Margaret laughed. "Well, that's the long-term plan. Short term, until we can start drumming up enough business and pay off our debts, we may have to put in more hours than that initially."

"Oh, yes, of course."

After a couple more hours of brainstorming and reviewing finances and logistics, Judy and Bob arrived.

"Hello, everyone. Boy, it's chilly out there with that ocean breeze. By the way, your Christmas decorations out on the wrought iron fence have come down. Did you guys know that?"

"What? Like they were torn down?" Liz rushed over to the window.

Margaret opened the front door and looked out. "No, we were not aware of that. Who would do such a thing? The house tour is only a couple hours away. We have to go fix it now."

Sarah, Margaret, and Liz rehung the white lights along the wrought iron fence.

"You know, I don't know how I missed this when I got here. I guess I just wasn't looking," Sarah said as she maneuvered the lights in a weaving pattern between the fence posts.

"I have an idea of who probably did this," Liz said with her eyes squinted towards the nasty neighbors.

Margaret stopped and looked over at their house. "Well, I'd like to think it wasn't them, but you may be right. We are not Henry and Barbara. Not sure why they have it out for us."

Margaret looked towards the neighbors' second-floor window and saw a man's head looking through the curtains at them. He immediately moved away from the window once he saw Margaret had noticed him.

"Well, it appears they're watching us. I just saw the man looking at us through the window upstairs," Margaret said through her teeth.

"Let's just get these lights hung and get back inside. I don't have the time or desire to deal with them right now," Liz said.

"Are the kids still watching movies in the basement?" Margaret checked her watch. "I feel like we've lost track of time. The house tour is only two hours away."

"Yeah, they're having a ball in that basement. They're watching movies and playing games," Liz said as she finished up hanging the lights.

Minutes later, as they headed back in the house, Dave's truck pulled into the driveway.

"Hey, ladies. It's the big day, eh? You all ready for the fun that's about to ensue?" Dave said with a big smile on his face.

"You could say that. We just had to rehang these lights on the fence that *someone* tore down," Liz said while looking over at the neighbor's house.

Dave shook his head. "Oh, jeez. That's not good. Well, let's not let it spoil the day."

They walked inside and Margaret stopped in her tracks. "I just realized something. The annual West Cape May Christmas Parade is today and it starts at 5 p.m., the same time as the house tour. Not only that, the annual Christmas tree lighting ceremony is at 7 p.m., at the old historic hotel. I forgot they changed the date for that this year due to the weather. We aren't going to be able to make it to either of them. The girls look forward to it every year. I must have forgot, with how busy we've been."

"Oh, my. I forgot, as well. The boys love it too. Not to mention, Greg and I look forward to it every year. It's a tradition," Liz said.

Just then, Judy walked into the room. "Well, I could run the house tours with your aunts. They will be here shortly and they wanted to be here for it anyway. We know all about the history of the house and where everything is, so it would work perfectly."

Liz looked over at Margaret. "Well, she has a point. We all don't really need to be here for the tours, right?"

Margaret thought for a moment and looked over at Judy. "Are you sure you're OK doing it?"

Judy laughed. "Margaret, I know this house like the back of my hand from being here so much and helping out. Your aunts love being here. It's a win-win. We will have a ball doing it!"

Margaret smiled and sighed. "OK, OK. We'll let you guys do the house tour, but I need you to call me immediately if anything goes wrong or you need help."

Judy looked through the top of her glasses at Margaret. "Your uncles and your father will also be here. We have all the help we will surely need. You all go out and enjoy yourselves. You've been working yourselves into the ground with this B&B. You deserve it."

"Perfect! Well, let's get all of the Christmas lights turned on and do a quick run-through with Mom. Then, how about we grab something quick to eat before the parade? I know the kids will be hungry," Liz suggested as they walked from room to room plugging in the lights.

"Sounds great," Margaret said.

They finally made their way out of the house with everyone bundled up. The whole gang was together, well everyone except Greg. He had been exhausted from his job and doing daddy overtime with the boys.

They stopped for a quick bite, and made their way to get a good spot up front for the annual Christmas parade. The event had been a holiday tradition in Cape May for more than fifty years. Margaret and Liz grew up going to it. They loved bringing their kids to it every year.

Dave spread out a couple big blankets alongside the curb for everyone, then sat down. Margaret sat in front of him and leaned her body into him while he wrapped his arms around her. The kids sat along the curb anxious to see everything up close.

"I really wish Greg were here," Liz said sitting on the second blanket all by herself while Sarah chatted with kids on the curb.

"Did you call him? Tell him to meet us here. You guys only live right down the road," Margaret said, cozy beneath Dave's warm arms.

Liz looked ahead. "I don't think he's too happy with me right now. He'll probably not want to come."

Margaret looked at Liz with a sad face, just as the parade started. Firetrucks, theatrical dancers, and brightly lit festive floats came down the street before them. Marching bands from different schools in New Jersey donned Santa hats and played Christmas songs as the crowd clapped and sang along.

"This parade always puts me in a Christmas mood," Margaret said while looking up at Dave.

Dave smiled and squeezed his arms a little tighter around her. "I have to agree; we also attended this parade as kids. I wish my family were here for this."

Margaret thought for a moment. "They're coming for Christmas, right? Where are they staying?"

Dave shrugged. "Last I heard, they hadn't found a suitable place. Of course, my place is way too small to host them."

Margaret turned to Liz and yelled out over the parade music. "Liz! Do we have any bookings for Christmas Eve or Christmas Day yet?"

Liz yelled back. "No. None. Not even the day before Christmas Eve. Why?"

Margaret smiled. "Well, make those days unavailable. I want Dave's family to stay at the B&B—no charge, of course. They're coming in from out of town. Plus, we should take that time off to be with our families anyway. Maybe we can all be together at the B&B for Christmas?"

Liz thought for a moment. "That could work out nicely."

Dave looked at Margaret, stunned. "Are you sure? That would be incredible. You do remember I said my mother was a little direct, right? I'm just warning you."

"Oh, that's fine. I'm sure everything will be great. Just let them know the details," Margaret said while nestling back into her cozy spot on Dave.

The parade having ended, the group hustled over to the tree lighting ceremony, and it looked like everyone else at the parade had migrated there too. The place was packed, as usual. The old hotel looked like a winter wonderland, fully decorated and lit brightly with Christmas lights. In the middle stood the huge unlit Christmas tree. They first made their way inside to the ballroom for some caroling with the choir, which the kids loved.

Finally, it was time to make their way out for the tree lighting ceremony.

Margaret leaned down and threw her arms around her girls. Liz did the same with the boys. Sarah and Dave chatted as they all waited.

The countdown started amongst the crowd.

Ten ... nine ... eight ... seven ...

Just then, Greg walked up behind Liz, which took her by surprise.

Liz jumped and hugged Greg. "You're here! I'm so glad. It's just not the same doing all of these Christmas things without you."

The boys ran over and hugged Greg too.

Greg stood with a smile on his face and his favorite arms wrapped around him as the countdown continued.

Six ... five ... four ... three ... two ...one!

The lights flashed on, illuminating the beautiful thirty-foot blue spruce full of thousands of colorful Christmas lights and a large star which perched atop it.

Everyone *oohed* and *aahed* and took photos. It was magnificent.

"Let's grab some hot chocolate and browse the vendors at the shopping village," Margaret suggested.

Liz sighed and wrapped her arms around Greg again while following behind Margaret, Dave, and the kids. "Are you mad at me still? I know I haven't been home as much. I guess I didn't realize how much this B&B would monopolize my time. Margaret and I have already discussed hiring people to help us so we have more time for our lives. We are both trying to work it out."

Greg laughed. "Yeah, I guess you could say I was mad. I've been overworked and stressed with my job, and I guess I felt like my feelings weren't being acknowledged through all of this. However, I did have time to sit and think about it today. You're just trying to do your best for the family, and I was being a little needy. I'm glad to hear you're hiring people. I think once you and Margaret figure out a routine that works, it'll be smooth sailing."

Liz pecked him on the cheek, then Greg grabbed her hand and kissed it while smiling.

"I'm so glad you talked to me about how you felt. I know

sometimes that isn't so easy for you. If it makes you feel any better, we've already hired Sarah to work at the B&B."

"Oh, really? Well, I hope I won't be hearing about any crazy food fights in there," Greg said with a chuckle.

They grabbed some hot chocolates and browsed the brightly lit shopping booths full of all different kinds of Christmas items and sweet treats. The kids were engrossed with a toy booth full of handmade animals held up by strings attached to a wooden stick. When they moved the sticks side to side, the animals appeared to walk.

Afterwards, they made their way to the firepits, arranged their blankets around one, and shared the pumpkin bread they'd bought from a vendor, passing it back and forth.

"I saw a gingerbread decorating table back over there. Would the kids want to go?" Sarah asked.

Liz and Greg's boys and Margaret's daughters all jumped up with pumpkin bread still in their mouths and raced over to Sarah with excitement.

Margaret chuckled. "I'm guessing that's a yes. We'll be here when you're finished."

Margaret looked back over at Liz and Greg. Liz leaned into Greg who had his arm around her, and they were laughing and giggling in their own little world, oblivious of what was going on around them.

Dave laid on the blanket facing Margaret holding his head up with his arm. "Well, it looks like Liz and Greg worked things out."

Margaret looked over at them again. "Yeah, it sure does, and I'm glad. I hate to see Liz unhappy … and Greg, for that matter."

Dave gazed across the lawn before his eyes settled on something. "I think I see Sandy over there by that firepit."

Margaret rolled her eyes. "I'm guessing Paul is over there too? Sometimes I hate how small of town it can be here."

Dave discretely searched the area. "Nope, I don't see Paul. I do see Will and Michelle though."

"Hmm ... that's odd. Maybe he's off getting hot chocolate or something. I'm sure the girls would love to run into him," Margaret said.

Dave surveyed the crowd and finally saw someone walking over towards Sandy. "Oh, there he ... oh, wait. That's not Paul."

Another man, taller than Paul and with blond hair, cozied up next to Sandy and pecked her on the cheek as he handed her a hot chocolate.

"Well, it looks like she has a new boyfriend. That's interesting but not surprising, knowing her track record. Maybe Paul actually took my advice that night we talked at the B&B."

Margaret fixed her eyes across the lawn at Sandy. "I sure hope so."

A group text message came through on both Margaret's and Liz's phone at the same time, pulling Margaret out of her reverie. Judy had sent a photo of a long line wrapped around the block of people waiting to do the house tour.

You two wouldn't believe the amount of people that are lined up to do the house tour. A lot of them have mentioned the article in the paper today. They couldn't wait to see the secret attic room and stairwell in the closet. I've already got a couple hundred more e-mails and addresses from our sign-in book. We are having a ball hosting the house tour tonight. Your aunts have already asked if they can do it again next year. Your father and uncles had a great time watching old westerns in the basement movie room. They're still down there now, but asleep and snoring loudly.

CHAPTER NINE

By the following weekend, The Seahorse Inn was fully booked. Their first guests arrived on Friday for their weekend stays full of Christmas cheer in Cape May.

Margaret and Liz were excited and ready, having cleaned each room an extra time before adding final touches of printed Cape May Christmas itineraries and gourmet chocolates on the bedside tables. Everything came together nicely, and they even figured out a schedule that worked for them, Sarah, and their newly hired house cleaner for the time being. They planned on eventually hiring more help after some time of settling in and figuring out what worked best for them and the B&B.

The first couple to check in, Jane and Norm, had been regulars back when Henry and Barbara ran the B&B. They were in their early seventies and adorable. They smiled a lot and talked about their grandchildren whenever they got the chance. They hadn't been to Cape May in some time, and we're delighted to finally be back at their favorite B&B.

The next guests to arrive were Fiona and Owen, a middle-aged couple from Ireland. They traveled to Cape May every year in December to visit relatives for a month and decided a weekend away from their large family was needed this time around. Their accents were thick, and they were loud and hysterical. They promptly asked where the closest Christmas-themed pub was upon checking in at 3 p.m.

With Fiona and Owen, came Fiona's sister and husband, Leona and Ronan. They were also visiting from Ireland and let the kids stay with their local family while they took a relaxing weekend away. They were even louder than Fiona and Owen and laughed at just about anything anyone said, funny or not.

Next, a quieter couple from Oregon, Jeff and Lauren, arrived with little fanfare. They were very much into ghosts and other paranormal type stuff and were intrigued by the secret attic room they'd read about online. They had already planned out their visits to all of the many supposed haunted places in Cape May for their long weekend stay.

When all the other guests had been checked in, the last couple arrived two hours later. Bernie and Bonnie were a quirky couple in their sixties who lived in upstate New York on an alpaca farm and owned a health food shop. Bernie's brown hair was long and braided, and Bonnie's was even longer. Their first question was about where they could find some incense.

Margaret and Liz loved everything about the Seahorse's opening day. They adored talking with and getting to know all of their interesting guests. It felt like a huge family get-together, except with brand-new family members who had interesting stories to share that they'd never heard before.

Besides breakfast, they offered a tea hour around 4 p.m. that included homemade baked goods, hot or cold tea, and fresh fruit. At 5:30, they did a wine-and-cheese hour full of colorful charcuterie boards, different kinds of cheeses, vegeta-bles, dips, and of course, wines. The guests came and went at their leisure. It made for the perfect amount of time for some light appetizers and relaxing before the guests went off to their dinner reservations. It also helped with getting all of the guests to mingle and get to know each other, something Liz and Margaret encouraged at the Seahorse. At 8 p.m., they would hold a movie night in the basement's movie theater, showing old Christmas movies.

Around 6:30pm, Sarah showed up to work her first shift. Margaret and Liz planned to head home to their families, but wanted to stay all the way through on their first weekend.

"So, I think some people were heading up the sidewalk as I walked in," Sarah said, hanging her coat up in the closet.

"That's odd. We're fully booked," Liz said as she opened the front door.

A couple in their sixties stood on the porch holding a wrapped lemon loaf and a bouquet of flowers in their hands. "Hi, there. We're Susan and Mike, your neighbors a couple doors down. We run The Sand Dune Inn. We've been meaning to come over and introduce ourselves, but have been pretty busy," Susan said.

"How lovely. Come on in. Take your coats off. So nice to meet you," Liz said as she grabbed their coats and the gifts they'd brought.

"Great to meet you! This is perfect timing too. Our guests have settled in and most of them have gone out to dinner, so it's pretty quiet right now. I'm sure it will be busy once our movie hour starts," Margaret said joyfully.

Margaret and Liz gave them a tour around the house, chatting all the while and getting to know the friendly neighbors. Meanwhile, Sarah prepared some fun snacks for the Christmas movie, striking just the right combination of classic theatre fare and festive seasonal treats.

"Well, we'd best be going. It was great meeting you," Mike said as they donned their coats.

"Yes, it's wonderful having nice neighbors," Margaret said while chuckling.

Susan stopped abruptly while buttoning her coat and looked over at Margaret and Liz. "Have you been having issues with the owners of Morning Dew Cottage, by chance?"

Margaret sighed. "Actually, yes. They seem to hate us for no reason. We've heard they didn't get along with Henry and Barbara, our Uncle Lou's parents. We were given the Seahorse by our Aunt Mary and Uncle Lou."

Mike unzipped his coat, hanging it back in the closet and Susan unbuttoned the very buttons she'd just done up.

"Look, how much do you know about what went on between them?" Mike asked hesitantly.

"Just that they didn't like each other, really," Liz said, concern and curiosity creeping in.

"Well, I guess we can stay a little longer. I think someone needs to fill you in on the details since you're dealing with the aftermath. We were here for all of it, and were friends with both couples. There are two sides to that story, and I think you're only hearing one."

Sarah poked her head in from the kitchen, curious to hear what Mike and Susan were about to divulge.

"Do you have a place away from the guests where we can discuss? I certainly don't want anyone else hearing this," Susan said.

Margaret thought for a moment and directed them to the basement. "Yes, down there. The home theater has plenty of room and privacy for us to talk, and the guests won't be coming down until close to eight o'clock."

They made their way into the basement and got comfy on the couches. Margaret turned some light music on the speakers to drown out their conversation just in case.

"Well, first things first. Hugh and Betty are the neighbors we're referring to. They own The Morning Dew Cottage next door. They probably opened their B&B a little before Henry and Barbara did," Susan said.

"Oh, that's right. John told us their names," Liz confirmed.

Susan rolled her eyes. "We love John and Rose, but they only know Henry and Barbara's side of the story."

Susan continued on. "Anyway, believe it or not, Henry and Barbara used to be good friends with Hugh and Betty for many years. It wasn't always nasty between them. They hung out all of the time. They even invited each other to one another's family get-togethers, and so forth."

Margaret gasped. "What? Well, *that* is shocking."

Mike, who'd been quietly listening from the recliner across the room chimed in. "Yep, it's true. Hard to believe, right?"

Susan nodded at Mike and looked back over at Margaret and Liz. "Well, one December years ago, we had a big snow-storm. It was something like a foot and a half of snow. Hugh had been using his snowblower on the driveway for hours. Little did he know the snow he was blowing was drifting right onto Henry and Barbara's driveway—which, as you know, is on the other side of the wrought iron fence. Henry came outside and saw what was happening, and wasn't happy about it. What initially started as a discussion between them, turned into an all-out nasty argument, and I'm talking *nasty*. The police ended up being called, and that was just the first of many times they were called months after that."

"Are you kidding me? This all started over a snowblower? Over a miscommunication? It sounds like they both needed to get their egos in check," Liz said, shocked.

Margaret threw her hands up and started laughing. "This is insane."

Mike sat up from his recliner. "You're telling us. We got stuck in the middle of it because we were friends with all of them. It was awful. Both couples felt we were taking sides if we even talked to the other couple. We ended up having to distance ourselves from all of them. It pretty much ruined our friendships with them."

Margaret shook her head. "What does this have to do with us though? That's what I'm not getting."

Susan cleared her throat. "Well, there's more. Did you happen to find Hugh and Betty's guest books when you acquired this B&B?"

Margaret and Liz both stood up abruptly. "Are you kidding me? Those guest books are *theirs*?" Liz yelled out.

"Well, before you jump to conclusions, Henry and Barbara did employ the use of guest books as well. Did you take a look to see?" Susan asked.

Margaret marched up the basement steps. "I'll grab the guest books and the remaining box that we haven't opened yet. I need to know if we've inadvertently poached our neighbors' guests."

Liz looked back over at Susan. "We found the guest books hidden away in the attic bedroom. We were wondering why they were so hard to find."

Susan shook her head. "They were hidden on purpose. They didn't want Hugh and Betty to get ahold of them."

Just then, Margaret marched back down the steps with two boxes. One with the guest books they'd already looked through and another that was still taped shut. "Well, here they are. Maybe you can tell us if these guest books were ours or theirs."

Susan grabbed the two guest books and studied them. "Well, these two definitely belong to The Seahorse Inn. See, the cover has the logo of the horse with the wreath covered with seahorses around its neck. The address is also printed inside, and the guests reference the B&B by name."

Liz fell back into her chair. "That's a relief. We sent out e-mails and postcards to everyone in those two books about the reopening of the Seahorse. Had those been someone else's guest books, I would have felt horrible."

Margaret pulled the tape off the sealed box and opened its lid to reveal more books that were full of news articles popping out of the tops of them.

"What in the world is all of this?" Margaret asked, pulling everything out of the box.

Susan gasped while reaching to grab two thick books. "Here they are. These are Hugh and Betty's guest books. So, it's true. Henry and Barbara had them all along."

Liz and Margaret were confused. "Why would they steal guest books?"

Susan shook her head. "You must understand that back then, these guest books were all the innkeepers had in terms of organizing their guests' information. It was important for keeping the business afloat. As you know, they had a line for the guest's name, residential address, phone number, and e-mail address, when people started using them more, and any comments. If you didn't copy your guest book information onto the computer or make photo copies, it was considered risky. Nowadays, everything is mostly done online and saved."

Mike walked over and sat on the floor next to the boxes. "So, what we were told happened was this … Before the snowblower argument, they had all gotten together at Henry and Barbara's, and Betty, for some reason, had the guest books with her. She laid them on the coffee table while they all hung out. Later, when Hugh and Betty left, they forgot to take their guest books with them. Foolishly, they hadn't recorded any of their guests' information anywhere else. Almost all of their past guests' information was in those books. The snowblower fight happened days after that, and Henry refused to return them out of spite. He even hid them from Barbara so she would never be tempted to return them."

"Well, *we* need to return them promptly. Henry should have returned them. It was the right thing to do," Margaret said, standing up.

"Hold on. There's more …" Susan said as she pulled the articles out of the books and read them.

"More?!" Liz gasped.

Susan piled all of the articles and pieces atop one another. "These newspaper clippings … they're crime reports from every time the police were called on either them or Hugh and

Betty. The rivalry got pretty nasty. Henry and Barbara's B&B flourished while Hugh and Betty started struggling with theirs. The Morning Dew Cottage was their only income, and they had already been in dire straits with booking enough guests prior to all of this mess. Hugh and Betty became angry all of the time. They were different people. They started sabotaging The Seahorse Inn any chance they got. That's when the police started to get called regularly. It was an absolute nightmare. That was right about the time that we had to cut ourselves off from all of them."

Margaret threw her head into her hands. "This is so childish and stupid. I can't wait to return these books. We need to make things right."

"We definitely do." Liz agreed.

Susan pulled out one last article from the book and laid it on the floor. "There's one last thing I should mention. The final blow was when Henry and Barbara did an interview with the local paper—that paper isn't around anymore—but in the article they discussed their nasty rivalry with Hugh and Betty and The Morning Dew Cottage, and the reporter told everything from their side. It tarnished Hugh and Betty's reputation for years after that. Not only had they lost all of their guests' information, but then they'd been boycotted. Their business plummeted, and they were forced to find other jobs while they tried to bring their B&B back to life."

Mike got up and headed towards the steps. "And there you have it! That's the story. If you want to make nice with the neighbors, I suggest you apologize on behalf of your Uncle Lou's parents and return those books, though I'm not sure how much good that will do now. We definitely must be going now. Let us know how it all turns out."

Susan sighed and started making her way up the basement steps behind Mike. "I really hope you can make peace with them. The whole situation broke our hearts. There wasn't any side that we agreed with. Both couples were out of line.

However, I do agree that they should have never kept those guest books."

"Oh, rest assured we will definitely try and make things right," Margaret said as she followed them up the steps.

They said their goodbyes to Mike and Susan and made their way back into the kitchen.

Sarah had just finished preparing all the movie munchies and glanced over at Margaret and Liz. "So I heard every word, and I'm in shock."

Margaret gasped. "You did? Did any guests hear?"

Sarah laughed. I was the only one down here. Don't worry. I can't believe the drama that went on between your Uncle Lou's parents and the neighbors next door. No wonder they're so nasty."

Liz sighed. "You're telling us. Now we have to be the ones who apologize and return the guest books, when it should be them. We barely even know Henry and Barbara. I think we met them twice when were in grade school."

Margaret laughed. "Figures we would get thrown into this mess. Now I see why Aunt Mary never got along with them."

Sarah smiled. "Off topic, but can I say how much I love working here already? Who knew I would love making delectable snacks so much? Check out my scrumptious spread in the kitchen and my fancy coffee bar that I made for the 8 o'clock movie later.

Margaret and Liz followed her into the kitchen, and looked over the spread that seemed to be fit for a king.

"Wow, you've outdone yourself, Sarah," Margaret said and gave her a high five.

Liz quickly loaded up a plate for herself. "I've barely eaten anything today. It's been too busy and exciting to find time."

Margaret, also grabbed a plate. "Hearing all of that drama made me famished. Who knew my heart rate could rise that high during a story about bed-and-breakfasts."

Sarah laughed. "OK, you two. Hurry up because the

guests are going to be here any minute, and seeing the hosts eating their movie snacks is a little awkward."

Margaret and Liz laughed while quickly trying to eat what was on their plates.

"I'm going to spruce up the home theater for our guests and get the movie cued up," Margaret said as she made her way into the basement.

Sarah adjusted a vase of flowers in the kitchen and chuckled. "You two need to go home to your families. I've got this."

CHAPTER TEN

The B&B was loud the next morning with a cacophony of pre-breakfast sounds filling the house. Coffee being poured, silver-ware clanging while stirring in the mugs, and the din of conversation and laughing abounded. Margaret and Liz were in the throes of preparation for the inn's first breakfast. The guests were previously instructed to sit across from another guest they didn't know. It was a little trick the sisters had learned to get everyone talking—an icebreaker of sorts, and it worked. They had couples sitting in the kitchen and the dining room, but the dining room was by far louder and chattier.

The Ireland couples, Fiona and Owen and Leona and Ronan, all arrived a little late to breakfast. They laughed loudly the entire time they drank their coffees at the dining room table.

Bernie and Bonnie smiled, not quite sure what could be so funny so early in the morning. "Care to share what's so funny? I could use a laugh," Bernie said as he threw his long braid behind his back and took a sip of coffee.

Fiona laughed so hard she could barely get any words out. Leona stepped in. "Well, since my sister, Fiona, can't contain herself long enough to tell the story, I will," Leona said while trying not to laugh.

"You see, last night we all stayed out a bit late while having a bit of fun, if you know what I mean. When we got back and went to our rooms, Ronan and I were pretty knackered. We changed out of our clothes, turned all the lights out, and hopped into bed for a good night's rest. About an hour later, I woke up having to go to the toilet. In the dark, I felt around for the doorknob, and don't you know, I ended up in the hallway instead, while the door to the room shut and locked behind me. I banged on the door to our room for what felt like ten minutes. I'm surprised I didn't wake all of you."

Norm cleared his throat, then took a sip of his coffee.

Leona giggled and looked at Norm. "I'm so sorry, did I wake you, sir?"

Norm chuckled. "You can call me, Norm. But … maybe just a little. It's OK. I fell right back to sleep."

Jane nudged Norm underneath the table, feeling a little embarrassed, then looked over at Leona and smiled. "Go on, dear. I love a funny story."

"Well, Ronan is the heaviest sleeper I know. A freight train could go right through our room, and he would not even stir. I kid you not! All that banging did nothing. On top of it all, I was not dressed to be out in the hallway, if you know what I'm saying. So, I banged on Fiona and Owen's door. They finally let me in, and I spent the rest of the night curled up in the chair they have in their room. I can't even turn my neck now from the way I slept."

Bonnie laughed. "Well, that sounds like a very eventful evening."

Leona made one loud laugh. "Oh, it gets better. This morning when I made my way back to our room, the door was cracked open, the TV was blaring, and I found Ronan asleep in the tub. He'd apparently sleepwalked in there, and then gotten comfy in the tub. Somehow, he opened the door to the room in the process."

Ronan looked over at Fiona hysterically laughing and practically falling out of his chair. The rest of the table succumbed to the contagious laughter.

Everyone finally simmered when Margaret and Liz walked out carrying stacks of cranberry pancakes and generous portions of frittatas.

Owen looked over at Jeff and Lauren while taking a bite of pancakes. "I saw you two coming in pretty late last night. Care to share?"

Lauren chuckled and took a sip of coffee. "Well, we have a bit of an interesting story ourselves. We love visiting haunted places and going on tours. We were drawn to The Seahorse Inn when we read the story about the secret attic room. It intrigued us."

Everyone at the table nodded and kept eating.

Lauren looked over at Jeff. "We had a great night exploring around the town, getting to see these old haunted places. We called it a night, and got into bed, and ... some really weird stuff started happening. At first, there was banging, but we've come to find out that was just you," Lauren said, turning to look at Leona.

Jeff interrupted. "But after the banging there was more. We heard things in our room opening and closing. We couldn't see anything because the lights were out. We turned the lights on, but didn't see anything. Nothing looked out of place. We turned off the lights and drifted off to sleep only to be awoken by the same sound again. That time, we didn't bother trying to look and just went right back to sleep. This morning, we woke up and our dresser drawers were all pulled out."

Everyone at the table froze; a fork dropped, mouths hung open.

Then Fiona interjected, "Now we all know it was just Ronan sleepwalking into your room. Come on! The door to his room was open this morning. Some shenanigans definitely went down. It's obvious what happened here."

The table erupted in laughter while Ronan turned a bright shade of red and laughed along with them, covering his eyes and shaking his head.

Lauren, still laughing, looked over at Bonnie and Jeff. "What did you guys do yesterday? Any funny stories?"

Bonnie chuckled. "Our day was quaint. Nothing nearly as exciting as you all. We collected shells on the beach, found a fabulous vegetarian restaurant with the most exquisite food, and shopped some book stores. However, we did see something a little strange. There was someone in the next-door's upstairs window staring at us the entire time we sat on the front porch last night while listening to the ocean. I'm talking the entire time. We finally went inside because it was creepy."

Jeff and Lauren looked at each other. "I'm betting ghosts. Or did Ronan sleepwalk his way over there too?"

The table erupted in laughter again with people wiping tears away with their napkins.

Bernie looked over at Jane and Norm. "How about you two?"

Jane smiled. "Oh, we're just two grandparents enjoying a relaxing weekend. I'm afraid our day sounds rather boring compared to everyone's here."

Bonnie smiled. "Well, share anyway. I'd love to know."

Jane took a sip of coffee. "Well, we did our crossword puzzles, enjoyed the tea during wine-and-cheese hour, and then took a small walk down the street to look at the Christmas lights. We went to bed early."

The table nodded and smiled and continued eating.

Norm cleared his throat and chuckled. "Well, there was one thing that happened. During our walk, I somehow stepped in a giant pile of horse poo. How it got on the sidewalk, I have no idea?"

Everyone at the table was quiet. Several pairs of eyes

darted at each other, and in unison the table shouted, "It was Ronan!"

The table erupted in the loudest laughter yet. Guests who'd been sitting in the kitchen moved to the dining room to find out what was so funny. Margaret and Liz grabbed empty plates while laughing themselves. They'd heard most of the conversation from the other room.

Ronan stood up and took a bow. "Well, I'm glad to be the butt of all the jokes this morning. It's been an honor."

The table continued laughing, and everyone eventually made their way back to their rooms to get ready for the day.

Margaret and Liz finished cleaning up breakfast before taking a break to sit and relax in the basement. Just as Margaret sank down in a recliner, her cell phone rang. "Hi, Aunt Mary."

"Hi Margaret. I just wanted to check on you and Liz to see how the B&B is going. Is everything all right?"

Margaret sat up. "Oh, everything is going great right now. We have our first guests this weekend, and it's been so much fun so far. There is one thing though …"

"Oh? What's that, dear?" Aunt Mary said with a little concern.

Margaret sighed. "Do you know anything about the feud that Uncle Lou's parents had with their next-door neighbor?"

Aunt Mary gasped. "No! Not a clue. You've got to be kidding me. Though, I'm not surprised. They were never the nicest to me, hence, why I was never that fond of them."

"Well, the neighbors next door have been nothing but nasty to us, and we had no clue why either. But last night we got filled in—from other neighbors. Tuns out Uncle Lou's parents were friends with them and then got in a huge fight, things escalated and then culminated in Henry and Barbara refusing to return their guests books, which were of great importance to the neighbors. Then, Uncle Lou's parents did an interview for a newspaper article about the situation and utterly tarnished the neighbor's reputation and subsequently caused their B&B to lose tons of business."

"Oh, Margaret. I'm so sorry you two have been put in this awful situation. Had I known anything about it, I would have surely warned both of you or at least tried to fix it."

Margaret sighed. "It's OK. I've already decided that we're going to rectify as best we can tonight around dinnertime and try to apologize on behalf of Uncle Lou's parents."

Aunt Mary took a long pause. "Well, let me know of anything I can do to help."

"Will do, Aunt Mary. Talk soon," Margaret said as she hung up.

Liz looked over at Margaret. "So, we're doing this tonight. We're going to the neighbors? My stomach is in knots thinking about it."

Margaret reclined back in the chair. "You're telling me. I'm thinking after Sarah gets here, we'll head over."

* * *

Around dinnertime, after Sarah showed up to take over the shift, Margaret and Liz grabbed the guest books and walked next door. Before they even made it to the top step of The Morning Dew Cottage, a woman abruptly opened the door and peered out at them.

Margaret jumped back a little. "Oh, hi. It's your neighbors from next door. I just wanted to—"

"What are you doing on our porch? Who said you could come over here?"

Liz squinted her eyes, her blood boiling over. "We're here to return these guest books of yours that we found. If you gave Margaret a second to answer, maybe you'd have found that out."

Margaret looked over at Liz with eyes widened and a look signally her to bring her tone down.

The woman was silent for a moment. Then, called for her husband. "Hugh! Come out here, please."

Hugh shuffled in from a back room and looked Margaret and Liz up and down. "Yes, Betty? What is it?"

Betty put her hand on his shoulder and looked over at Margaret and Liz. "These are our neighbors over at The Seahorse Inn. They've found our guest books and brought them back."

Hugh scoffed. "Well, it doesn't do any good now. We could have used them many years ago."

Margaret interrupted. "Look, we are both just finding out what happened between you two and Henry and Barbara years ago. We want to make things right."

Betty looked towards the ocean and sighed. "It's too late for that now. The damage is done, and it's not your place to apologize for someone else."

The sound of screeching tires out front had Margaret and Liz whirling around on the porch to see what was happening at the curb. Aunt Mary and Uncle Lou got out, and each opened the back door on their side of the car. They assisted two older-looking people out of the car and helped them walk up the steps to Morning Dew Cottage.

When they got onto the porch, the older couple immediately took a seat in one of the several chairs available while catching their breaths.

Betty folded her arms. "I can't believe this. First you send these women over to apologize and *now* you two show up?"

Henry and Barbara finally stood back on their feet and walked right up to Hugh and Betty. "We're here to lay this feud to rest. We just found out from our son that you two are now being nothing but nasty to Margaret and Liz, the new owners. What have they done to you?" Barbara said while adjusting her blouse.

Hugh looked away, slightly embarrassed. "We figured they

were your grandkids and knew everything. We assumed the entire family knew and had it out for us."

Aunt Mary shook her head. "That is not the case at all. Margaret and Liz are not related to Henry and Barbara. They are from my side of the family and have only met them once or twice, but that is beside the point."

Henry grabbed the guest books from Margaret and Liz and handed them shakily to Hugh. "Here. These are yours. I should have never kept them. I even hid them from Betty so she wouldn't return them. All of this was more my fault than hers. My temper took the best of me. I was hurt and angry that a friendship could go sour so quick. I apologize."

Hugh sighed and paused. "I apologize too. All of those spiteful things I did to get back at you … I was angry. One simple miscommunication ruined a friendship and even our business for some years."

Aunt Mary pulled a checkbook out of her purse and feverishly began writing. She ripped the check out and handed it to Betty and Hugh. "Here. Take it. This is for your past business losses due to what happened. I want this ended right now. No more nastiness. No more feuding. No more grudges."

Betty's eyes welled up with tears as she looked at the number on the check. "I can't accept that. It doesn't feel right."

Aunt Mary shoved the check in her hands. "I don't care. From what I heard, it sounds like you almost lost your business, and it took years to build it back up. Please take it. Don't worry, we can most definitely afford paying you this."

Hugh put his arms around Betty, and they graciously took the check. "Please, would you all come in for a cup of coffee or tea?"

Henry glanced at Barbara who gave him an approving nod. They all walked in, and though Margaret and Liz felt out of place, they still followed behind.

Hugh and Betty and Henry and Barbara talked quite a bit, catching up on everything that had happened over the years since they'd last been friends. Uncle Lou and Aunt Mary chatted most of the time with Margaret and Liz about the B&B and Christmas while Henry and Barbara had their time to make amends.

Betty got up to answer a knock at the door and came back with Judy who was looking for Margaret and Liz.

"Hi, I hate to bother you all, but Margaret and Liz, I think Sarah might need some help next door."

"What do you mean?" Margaret asked.

"Well, I stopped by to see how everything was going, and it looks like all of the guests had a little too much wine and cheese and are having the loudest game of cards known to man."

"Mom, it's totally fine," Margaret laughed. "They are just a loud, jovial bunch. You should have seen how they all made friends with each other during breakfast."

Judy wiped invisible sweat off her forehead. "Well, that's good. I wasn't quite sure."

Henry, Barbara, and Hugh and Betty found the humor too. "Oh, we remember quite well having guests like that. They brought the party wherever they went. It reminds us of our son, Lou," Barbara said while snickering."

Hugh looked down at his shoes. "I guess I should mention … you remember our son, Steven?" Henry and Barbara nodded. "We haven't heard from him in years. We had an argument and have been estranged ever since. It breaks our hearts. It seems we are terrible at making amends with others."

Barbara took Hugh and Betty's hands and squeezed from across the table. "I'm so sorry."

Margaret and Liz got up from their seats. "Well, I'm glad we finally have some peace between us. Hugh and Betty, please let us know if you need anything. We'd be glad to help. Are you two booked up for Christmas with guests?"

Betty stood from her seat. "We are not, dear. It'll be just us here. This isn't just a B&B, it's also our home, so we're always here."

Liz thought for a moment. "Well, our family is having Christmas at the Seahorse this year. We'd like for you two to join us."

Betty's eyes welled up with tears again. "Oh, that would be lovely. We get so lonely sometimes. Most of our family lives across the country, and we never hear from our son. We have grandkids that we never see."

Judy put her arm around Betty. "Well, I'll be there with my husband, Bob. I would love to see you two for Christmas. The more the merrier!"

Margaret turned to Aunt Mary and Uncle Lou. "You two are more than welcome to come, as well as Henry and Barbara. Consider it an open house for Christmas!"

CHAPTER ELEVEN

Two and a half weeks went by with solid bookings and many events at the Seahorse. By Christmas Eve, Margaret prepared for Dave's family to arrive in the morning for their stay at The Seahorse Inn. The B&B wasn't booked with guests again until after Christmas, making it fully available for family festivities. Margaret and Liz couldn't wait to partake in a little time off with their families and friends. This included Dave's family, whom Margaret would be meeting for the first time.

Paul had their daughters for Christmas Eve day, and was bringing them back over in the evening. Judy and Bob planned to come over in the evening, as well as Liz, Greg, and their sons, along with some aunts, uncles, cousins, Sarah, and a few other straggler friends who didn't have any plans. It was going to be a packed house ... or B&B, rather.

In the early morning light, Margaret took her mug of hot coffee onto the porch and gazed out past the dunes towards the ocean. A slight breeze lifted the hair off her neck. She took a gulp of coffee and inhaled deeply, closing her eyes and letting herself fully enjoy this moment of peace. She was alone at the Seahorse, everyone else busy with other obligations. She glanced over and saw John and Rose sitting on their porch and waved. Then, she glanced in the other direction and saw Hugh and Betty, so she waved to them as well. Finally, there was peace among the neighbors. It was truly a Christmas miracle.

Inside, she had been baking some different breads. She loved to have some ready for Christmas and also to give away to the neighbors. Two of her favorites this time of year were lemon poppyseed bread and cranberry orange bread. It was a tradition to bring them to the neighbors in her neighborhood, but this year she'd extend the tradition to the neighbors near the B&B.

She looked over to see Dave's truck pulling into the driveway. He cheerfully hopped out, grabbing a few overloaded grocery bags from the back seat. He smiled when he saw Margaret as he walked up the steps, greeting her with a kiss while juggling the overstuffed bags in his arms.

"Merry Christmas Eve. I'm so excited to have my family here for the holidays for the first time in years. I ran out and bought some things to make."

Margaret smiled and followed him inside. "Oh, that's perfect. I just have some breads baking now. What are you thinking?"

Dave set the bags on the kitchen table to unload. "Well, I'm making a pumpkin pie—with real pumpkins—a pecan pie, and I got some ingredients for some of our traditional family side dishes for dinner."

"They're probably going to be pretty hungry when they arrive around lunchtime. I have a pot of homemade vegetable soup cooking and some little appetizers I can put out," Margaret said as she helped him put the grocery items away.

Dave abruptly stopped, looking at Margaret with a huge smile on his face. "You're amazing. Do you know that?"

Margaret blushed and smiled. "Well, I try. I want everyone to be happy."

Noon rolled around quickly, and Dave's family slowly

started trickling in. First his two brothers, Mike and Shaun, with their wives, Jill and Julie, and their kids arrived. Then his two sisters in quick succession: Beth with her husband and four kids, followed by his younger sister Irene, a single, childless, world traveler who's work on TV shows and films seemed very exciting. Aside from Mike, who lived in the area, the rest of them had moved to different parts of the country. They were all so happy and grateful to be back in Cape May for the holidays, and were thrilled to have a gorgeous B&B on the beach all to themselves.

Irene was tall and beautiful with blonde hair down to her shoulders and crystal-blue eyes. She'd started working on films a few years ago after abruptly leaving her teaching job, and was always working on something interesting. She immediately gave Margaret the tightest hug.

"I am *so* glad to meet you. Dave told me all about you, this B&B, and the garden and farm stand. You two seem great together, that's for sure."

Dave's brothers and wives all happily greeted Margaret, and already she loved his family. They were super sweet and interesting people. She'd worried that mixing her family with his might not work out, but now she was positive it would work out fine.

Dave's mom and dad arrived last, about thirty minutes after everyone else was settled in. Margaret waited at the door to the greet them and take their bags.

His mother heaved her bag onto her husband and marched up the steps. She was a short, round woman with wiry gray hair and dark eyes. She huffed and puffed as she walked up the steps empty-handed.

As his mother mounted the porch, having conquered the stairs, she immediately sighed. "Got enough steps to this place? I'm pretty sure that's all the exercise I need for the rest of the day."

Dave cleared his throat. "Mom, I'd like you to meet Margaret."

Margaret smiled and held out her arms to give her a hug. "It's so nice to meet you. I'm so glad you could come."

Dave's mom winced and reluctantly reciprocated Margaret's hug with a tap on the back. "Honey, you can call me Marge. Let's see this B&B of yours," she said as she walked past them inside.

Dave immediately ran out to the car to help his poor dad haul in all the luggage.

Marge looked the place up and down and laughed. "Well, this place sure is old as the dickens. I better not have a claw-foot tub in my room. We can't get in and out of them."

Margaret remembered what Dave had said about his mom being direct. "Oh, don't worry. Your room doesn't have a claw-foot tub. Would you like me to show you to your room?"

Marge walked into the living room, completely ignoring her question. "Has this fireplace been properly cleaned? If we're going to use it, I need to know. I have enough respiratory issues as it is."

Before Margaret could get a word out, Beth walked out from the kitchen. "Mom! Leave this poor woman alone. You've just arrived and you're already complaining."

Marge squinted her eyes and pulled her daughter in for a big hug. "It's nice to see you, Beth, but don't tell me what to do."

Beth rolled her eyes and mouthed her apology to Margaret as she left the room.

Dave and his dad, Roger, finally got the luggage up to the room and came back downstairs. Margaret was relieved as dealing with his mom was a little stressful.

Margaret walked into the kitchen. "Hey everyone, so there's homemade vegetable soup in the pot on the stove, and I put out some dips and other appetizers on the table. Help yourselves."

The group was famished and immediately grabbed plates and bowls to do just that.

Marge peered at the table. "I'm lactose intolerant. I can't eat half those things on the table."

Dave's brothers rolled their eyes and threw their heads back. Nobody was shy about their feelings about their mother.

Dave put his arm around Margaret. "Are you OK? I'm apologizing now on behalf of my mom. We all get annoyed with her. Trust me."

Margaret smiled. "It's OK. I'm sure it will all settle down."

Dave's family made their way to the dining room table to eat while Margaret made sure the appetizers were restocked in the kitchen.

From behind her, Dave pulled her in for a big hug. "It's Christmas. Don't worry about that. Sit and enjoy. I'll handle all of that."

Just then, a huge argument erupted in the dining room. Dave still had his arms around Margaret while they looked at each other, not sure whether to walk into the dining room or not. They decided to stay in the kitchen.

"I don't care what countries you've been to. You need to settle down, buy a house, and have some kids," Marge shouted across the table to Irene.

"Are *you* kidding me? So, I'm just supposed to live whatever life you tell me to live? My happiness doesn't matter? Unreal!" Irene shouted back.

Marge cackled. "Well, you need security in your life. How much do you have in savings? How much do you have put away for retirement? You're pushing forty, for Pete's sake!"

Irene laughed. "What I have put away in savings and retirement is none of your business. Frankly, what I do with my life"—she stood from the table—"isn't any of your business either."

"It's enough of this, Mom. You need to let off of Irene. Let her live her life and be done with it," Shaun said.

Marge rolled her eyes. "I will not. Don't get involved, son! When's the last time you even visited us in Florida?"

Beth shoved out of her seat, her fork clattering down on her plate. "Mom! That's it. We've all had enough of you and your antics. You and Dad retired and moved away to Florida and never visit anyone. You expect everyone to show up at your doorstep, but we have kids with school, soccer practices, and plays. We have jobs to go to. Our lives are ten times busier than yours. It's time you know how we feel. You want to see us, then *you* visit *us*. We can't make it to Florida every year. It's not feasible. And stop ragging on Irene—or anyone else. None of us are putting up with it anymore. And yes, I speak for all of us."

Marge folded her arms silently and stared her kids down one by one. "So, you *all* feel this way? Roger, did you hear this? They don't have time to visit us."

The entire roomful of Pattersons moaned in annoyance before their exodus to the kitchen.

Roger looked at Marge, stood up, and threw his napkin onto the table. "Marge, I've had enough. Only thirty minutes after arriving, and you've already insulted Margaret and started a fight with your kids. You'd better change your attitude real quick."

Marge's eyes welled up. "I'm just trying to have a conversation."

Roger pounded the dining room table out of frustration. "Stop making this about you. Go in and apologize to everyone in that kitchen right now. It's Christmas, and I'm not having any of this nonsense. Do you hear me?"

Marge sheepishly walked into the kitchen, stepping into the fray of her offspring busily helping to clean up. No one had noticed her entrance.

"I'm sorry," Marge said quietly as she stared at her feet.

"What's that, Mom? Did you say something?" Mike asked, turning around.

Marge raised her voice more. "I said I'm sorry," she said to the room, meeting the eyes of her children. "I was out of line. I apologize to all of you. Will you all forgive me?"

Beth walked over to Marge. "Of course. We love you. Just please be nicer to everyone. Can you do that?"

Marge, embarrassed, looked over at Roger who nodded at her. "Yes, you have my word."

Whether in a show of love or an attempt of passive-aggressive vexation, the entire family piled around Marge and gave her a big group hug. Intentional or not, the action proved to irritate her. "OK, that's enough! I can't breathe!" she bellowed.

Everyone let go and laughed, then made their way up to their rooms to change and settle in.

* * *

A couple of hours later, it was time to start cooking the big Christmas Eve feast. Liz, Greg, and the boys were the first to show up before the rest of Margaret's family arrived, followed by Sarah. It was a packed, lively house where conversations abounded from every room. The home theater played jolly Christmas movies, the fire crackled in the living room, and Christmas music played on the speakers. Some people were even bundled up outside getting a fire started in the pit that was brightly lit by the deck's white string lights. Dave's family engaged in conversation with everyone from Margaret and Liz's family. Everyone mingled with everyone. It was the perfect mash-up of families. Margaret couldn't have been more delighted.

Amid all the hustle and bustle, there was a knock at the door. Dave answered it, and Margaret's girls immediately engulfed him a huge hug then ran inside, excited to see their cousins.

Paul immediately extended his hand to Dave. "Merry

Christmas, Dave. While I have you here, I want to thank you for that talk we had a few weeks back. You really helped me decide what was best for me and the girls. I broke up with Sandy."

Dave smiled. "No problem, Paul. I'm happy that you're happy. Let me grab Margaret."

After Dave called for Margaret and she made her way through the noisy house that boasted a fantastic warm and joyful party, she smiled and extended her hand to her ex. "Hey, Paul. Merry Christmas. Did you have fun with the girls?"

Paul smiled. "I did. I brought them over to my mother's and we did lots of fun, Christmasy things. My mom said to tell you merry Christmas and thank you, by the way. She's actually in the car."

Margaret waved to the car, hoping she'd see her, then turned to Paul. "Why don't you two stay for dinner? We have plenty of food and more than enough room for both of you."

"That actually sounds great, but I told my mom I'd go with her to Aunt Donna's for Christmas Eve dinner. She's looking forward to it."

Margaret laughed. "Oh, I totally understand. Your Aunt Donna makes the best food. Well, we'll all be here tomorrow if you'd like to bring your mom and come for brunch and presents. You are both welcome to stay for dinner if you'd like."

"That's perfect, we don't have any solid plans. It'll be nice to be with the girls. I still have a few gifts to wrap up and give them too. My mom will love this. Well, we're running late, so I'll see you all tomorrow," Paul said as he made his way down the steps and back to the car.

Dave turned to Margaret and wrapped his arms around her and gave her a big kiss.

Margaret smiled. "What was that for?"

Dave gazed into her eyes. "Just grateful for this amazingly

compassionate and beautiful woman in my life. You did a good thing with Paul. I can't say I would ever do that with my ex."

Margaret laughed. "Well, it's two different situations, yours and mine."

They made their way back into the kitchen where people from Dave's side and Margaret's side were talking, laughing, and harmoniously preparing some dishes for dinner together. The buffet was set up on the kitchen island and counters, and the kitchen and dining room tables had lit tapered candles and beautiful place settings on them. A small kids' table was set with some cute Christmas place settings.

Dinner was served, and the B&B smelled amazing. It was the biggest food spread any of them had ever seen, with family-favorite dishes from both Margaret's side and Dave's. After dinner, there was a huge dessert spread.

Margaret pulled Dave aside. "Let's go for a Christmas Eve stroll, just you and me, before the rest of the traditional actives start."

Dave smiled and grabbed their jackets. "You bet. I'll tell everyone that we'll be back."

Margaret snagged a bag and loaded handfuls of her poppyseed lemon and cranberry loaves in it. "I just want to bring these over to the neighbors first."

Dave and Margaret made their way outside and were greeted with an extra chill in the air and the sound of the ocean waves, lapping gently.

Dave waited on the street as Margaret made her way to each of the neighbor's doors, handing them a loaf and wishing them a merry Christmas.

Afterwards, they walked to the Washington Street Mall, which was lit radiantly but completely empty and quiet—something neither of them were used to.

Dave put his arm around Margaret's waist. "What did the neighbors have to say when you handed them your goodies?"

Margaret smiled. "Well, John and Rose were delighted.

They didn't have plans tomorrow so they'll also be coming over for brunch and possibly staying longer. Hugh and Betty were happy to see me, and they'll be coming over tomorrow. They have already made amends with John and Rose, which was nice to hear. The rest of the neighbors, some I haven't even met until tonight, were so grateful and I look forward to us all getting to know them."

Dave smiled and kissed her on top of her head. "It will surely be a merry Christmas this year. It's quite romantic being the only ones out here in this wonderland on Christmas Eve, don't you think?"

Margaret's whole body warmed, she nodded, and took Dave's hand in hers. "Look at how elegantly decorated the store windows are. It's so magical this time of year. How did we get so lucky to live here?"

They made their way past the mall and down the streets lined with decorated bed-and-breakfasts, admiring each and every one when light, fluffy snow started to silently fall on them.

Dave laughed and held his hand out. "Snow? Is this really snow? We haven't had snow on Christmas in forever!"

Margaret laughed and spun around in the snow while holding her arms out. "This is incredible. Look at how grand the houses with Christmas lights look with the dusting on them."

Dave pulled out his phone and checked the weather. "Well, it looks like we're finally getting a white Christmas. I don't think I've seen one since I was a kid. Snow is in the forecast tomorrow."

Margaret looked over his shoulder at his phone. "Would you look at that? How did we miss *that*?"

Dave smiled, put his phone back in his pocket, and grabbed Margaret's hand. "Pretty sure all the hubbub around the holidays had us too busy to remember to check the weather. Do you want to walk the beach home? I've always wanted to walk the beach during a snowfall."

Margaret squeezed his hand and they walked down to the beach, as the moon shone bright, reflecting off the ocean, and the snow fell peacefully on them and the sand. The waves were placid, the air chilly and still.

They walked in silence along the beach, taking it all in before they arrived at the street where The Seahorse Inn stood. From the dunes, they gazed up at the B&B. The outside was brightly lit, and the inside glowed as well. Their family walked back and forth through the windows.

Dave wrapped his arms around Margaret. "What are the rest of the activities for the evening? We grew up not doing too much else except for dinner."

Margaret laughed. "Oh, get ready. It's a whole night of activities. First, we're doing a white elephant gift exchange. It gets pretty crazy and out of hand. Nobody knows what the wrapped gifts are, and it's a game where people can steal the gift from you and vice versa. Don't worry, I already got our gifts that we will be contributing. Your family is all in on it. Everyone plays! You should have seen my Uncle Tom last year. He had to have this one big gift. He kept stealing it back from whoever took it from him. I'm not sure what he thought it was, but it ended up being a ceramic goose! It was the funniest thing ever."

Dave laughed. "Well, that sounds right up my family's alley. Watch out, they can be super competitive."

Margaret laughed. "So can my family. This is going to be fun. Anyway, after the white elephant gift exchange, we gift the kids and adults Christmas pajamas. Everyone is supposed to wear them tonight for bed and into the morning. Then, we do a big family reading of *The Night Before Christmas* with the kids and put out milk, cookies, and carrots for Santa and the reindeer. After the kids go to bed, we finish wrapping all of the gifts, and put everything under the tree, which is usually a lot of laughs and fun. Then, a group of us adults will head out for midnight service at the beautiful old church in town, which starts earlier than midnight these days. It's breathtaking. Finally, we head to bed for a few hours of sleep before the kids wake us up at the crack of dawn, excited to open their gifts."

Dave smiled. "Well, we'd better get inside. I don't want to miss any of it."

CHAPTER TWELVE

At seven on Christmas morning, Margaret and Dave awoke to the sound of horse hooves clip-clopping outside the B&B. Margaret looked at the clock, stretched, and walked over to the window. The snow had continued on through the night and outside was a winter wonderland. Some empty horse carriages went by, which was peculiar as they usually weren't out on Christmas Day.

"Dave. Come look outside. It's absolutely magnificent," Margaret said, half-awake.

Dave put his slippers on, looked over her shoulder, and wrapped his arms around her. "Well, would you look at that. A white Christmas. The kids are going to be super excited."

Margaret and Dave had of course slept in the Christmas pajamas they'd gotten last night. Barging through the door moments later, the girls started jumping on the bed in their matching PJs.

"Let's go open gifts! We're ready!" Harper and Abby said, breath *whooshing* out of them from all of the jumping.

Margaret laughed. "OK, but we have to wait until everyone is downstairs to start opening them."

Just then, Liz and Greg peeked through the open door.

"Merry Christmas! We thought we you heard you guys. The boys woke us up an hour ago. Mom and Dad are already downstairs doing their crossword puzzles, and most of Dave's family is downstairs too. I put brunch in the oven already," Liz said, sipping her coffee.

Margaret yawned. "Merry Christmas, Liz and Greg! Did you see the snow? It's so beautiful."

Liz laughed. "Oh yes! The boys have already asked to go outside and play in it. I told them they have to wait until after we open gifts. On that note, do you think we're about ready?"

The girls jumped off the bed and ran down the stairs as fast as they could, barely containing their excitement.

Dave smiled at Margaret. "Since we're having people come over, I think I'm going to get my brothers to help me quickly shovel the sidewalks outside."

Margaret threw her arms around him. "Are you sure? Well, we'll wait until you're all done before we open gifts."

They made their way downstairs to the sounds of Christmas movies, happy chatter, a crackling fire, and the clatter of coffee being stirred with spoons. Everyone was awake. The house smelled like a mixture of pine tree and delicious baked casseroles. Judy and Dave's mom had already started getting the tables set for the traditional Christmas brunch after presents. All of the kids stared out the windows at Dave and his brothers shoveling, not sure whether to be more excited about opening gifts or playing in the snow.

Thirty minutes later, Dave and his brothers walked in, laughing, with snow all over them. Apparently, during the shoveling a snow ball fight ensued.

"When's the last time we all had a snowball fight?" Dave said to his brothers as he shook out his hair and took off his boots and jacket.

Shaun and Mike chuckled. "Not since when we were kids when Mike and I got you good on the farm," Shaun said while heading into the lively living room with Dave and Mike following behind.

Gathered together by the crackling fire, the two families gazed at a truck load's worth of gifts under the tree. There were a lot of people there, after all. Irene took charge of handing the gifts out, which she seemed to love.

Halfway through, there was a knock at the door. It was Paul and his mom, Elaine.

Judy greeted them and took their coats. Margaret made room for Paul and Elaine right by the girls and introduced them to Dave's family.

More knocks at the door came one after the other. Aunts, uncles, and cousins who'd already done gifts earlier at their own houses arrived to spend Christmas Day at The Seahorse Inn. Sarah was the last to arrive, bringing her parents with her.

Judy made an announcement after gifts were done being opened. "Brunch is just about ready if you all want to line up by the island. With this big family, we're doing buffet style as usual."

The kitchen smelled amazing. Liz, Julie, and Jill had already gotten all of the dishes laid out. There was baked French toast, quiche, hash brown casserole, baked apple oatmeal in a crock pot, fresh fruit, bacon and sausage, biscuits and gravy, and a few other things. Food seemed to be the love language for both families.

Judy looked at Liz, astonished. "How did you all get all of this cooked this morning?"

Liz glanced at Margaret and laughed. "Most of the adults stayed up late reminiscing, drinking, and laughing while watching old Christmas movies in the basement. We decided to just get everything made last night. Mostly everything just had to be popped in the oven this morning."

Irene laughed. "It was actually a lot of fun. I'm down for doing this again next year."

After the scrumptious brunch, the kids were ready to play

in the snow. The adults bundled up and went with them, fondly watching as snowmen and snow angels were made all over the front yard.

"Who is that?" Margaret said to Liz and Sarah when a car pulled up in the driveway.

A man got out of the car wearing a scarf, hat, and black peacoat and held two big paper bags full of presents.

Sarah gasped and ran over to him.

Margaret and Liz looked at each other and clasped hands. "It's Mark! I thought he wasn't going to be home until after Christmas?"

Dave shook Mark's hand and grabbed his bags just as Sarah jumped into his arms, tears welling up in her eyes.

"I didn't think I was going to see you for a few more weeks. I can't believe you're here!"

Mark laughed and spun her around. "They let me go home early for Christmas. I wanted to surprise you. Your parents clued me in on where to find you."

"They knew the whole time? Oh my gosh, I'm so happy to see you," Sarah said as she continued to hug him. "Come inside and get some brunch before it's put away."

Dave looked over at Margaret and smiled. Margaret felt so happy for Sarah in that moment. She was also happy to have someone she felt the same about.

The kids bombarded Dave with snowballs, climbing on him as he bent over to play with them. Suddenly, he abruptly stood up with an idea. "How about the guys take the kids sledding before dinner? I have the perfect spot in mind."

"Sure. Just be home by three. We're having an early dinner."

Back inside, Judy, the aunts, and some cousins were finishing cleaning up brunch when more knocks came at the door. This time, it was their neighbors, John and Rose and Hugh and Betty, with homemade dishes in their hands. Margaret hugged them and graciously took their dishes from them before Aunt Mary and Uncle Lou showed up with Uncle Lou's parents.

Everyone came together to get Christmas dinner underway. In addition to the copious amounts of side dishes brought or made by various friends or family members, there was also ham, turkey, mashed potatoes, sweet potatoes, asparagus, green bean casserole, hot rolls with butter, and macaroni and cheese.

The sledding crew returned with just enough time to get changed and cleaned up for dinner. Dave had already made his pies and side dishes in advance and was quite excited about putting them out for everyone.

Following dinner, Bob put the Christmas Day football game on in the basement, and many people followed him down there to watch.

Margaret nudged Dave. "Look at Sarah and Mark. They seem so in love. I've never seen her like this with anybody. She's *always* been single. I think her last boyfriend lasted six months and that was ten years ago."

Dave looked over and saw Sarah and Mark on the couch by the fire with her legs draped over his. They sipped after-dinner coffee, laughing and smiling while chatting quietly.

"See what I mean?" Margaret said with a smile.

Dave smiled. "I feel that way about you. You make every-thing wonderful. Christmas here has been something of a dream."

Margaret blushed and leaned her head against his chest. "Let's go put out desserts. I know you're excited about serving your pies."

The kids had taken over the living room, playing with the toys they'd received that morning while watching Christmas movies. Everyone was warmed up and ready for dessert.

Paul's mom, Elaine, pulled Margaret aside as dessert was being served. "You really hit the ball out of the park with this one."

Margaret smiled. "You're too kind, Elaine. This B&B really

is wonderful, and it's so nice to have our family and friends together."

Elaine laughed and turned to make sure nobody was listening. "I'm talking about your boyfriend over there. Dave, is it? I heard he baked these pies and put together that dreamy home theater in the basement? I saw you two canoodling, and I'm happy for you."

Margaret laughed. "You're too much, Elaine. By the way, I have someone I want you to meet. This is Dave's mom, Marge."

Margaret thought Elaine and Marge were two peas in a pod. Neither woman got along with Margaret at first, but now did. Maybe they'd get along with each other?

Elaine turned around to greet Marge. "I thought I recognized you. Didn't we go to high school together?"

Marge looked her up and down and smiled. "Elaine Wilder! What in the world? We played field hockey together. Your mom would throw the best post-game meals. I remember you!"

Margaret smiled and walked away. Dave glanced over at her and snickered, motioning to her that he saw what she did.

After dessert, the reminiscing at the dining room table commenced with Dave's family telling hysterical stories from when they were kids. Margaret and Liz's family interjected with their own stories, and everyone in the B&B was crowded around the table, laughing along.

When Dave's family started a Christmas dance party in the kitchen and living room, it got out of hand pretty quickly when Dave's brothers found some elf hats and did a choreographed dance that made everyone roll on the ground laughing. Absolutely hysterical.

Tired out from dancing, and after an insanely competitive game of Scrabble with the family, Dave and Greg pulled Margaret and Liz aside into the other room.

"Greg and I have a bit of a surprise for you two as part of your Christmas gifts," Dave said, grabbing their coats.

Greg motioned to the front door. "Go on. Take a look outside."

Liz and Margaret opened the front door to see a charming, festively decorated horse-drawn carriage outside with seating for four people.

"Is that for us?" Liz asked.

Dave and Greg smiled and nodded. "Are you two ready to go for a romantic Christmas ride around Cape May?"

When they got settled in the carriage, the driver happily introduced himself, and they rolled their way around the quiet beach town full of beautiful Christmas lights. The slow and steady *clip-clops* of the horse hooves on the pavement was so relaxing.

Dave grabbed a thermos of hot chocolate and cups out of a small bag he'd brought and poured some for everyone. Margaret took a sip, and felt her body warm from head to toe.

Greg handed out two blankets he'd grabbed, and they all got cozy. The stars and moon were clear and bright, and as they rode into town, they could see some of the other family celebrations going on through the windows of each of the old houses they passed.

Margaret sighed and leaned her head on Dave's shoulder. "It's so eerily quiet out here. Barely a car on the road. It feels like we have this town to ourselves tonight."

Liz held hands with Greg and snuggled up to him under their blanket, both of their eyes twinkling at the beautiful sights.

"This was such a wonderful gift you guys thought of," Margaret said.

Greg smiled. "Well, you two have been working so hard lately with this B&B, and we thought you'd both appreciate a nice, quiet carriage ride on Christmas Day."

Dave looked over at Margaret. "There's also one more surprise when we get back."

After the ride and arriving back to the B&B. they all exited the carriage, said their goodbyes to the driver, and made their way up the walkway to the Seahorse.

"The surprise is this way," Dave said, leading them to the back of the house.

Margaret and Liz smelled a campfire burning as they made their way to the back, and saw everyone bundled up roasting marshmallows and singing Christmas carols together.

Margaret and Liz laughed. "How fun is this? A carriage ride and a bonfire on Christmas Day. I think we found ourselves a new tradition."

"How was your carriage ride?" Judy asked from across the firepit.

"Absolutely wonderful."

Beth handed them some sticks and marshmallows, and they happily joined in the caroling and roasting of marshmallows.

Margaret looked over to see Hugh and Betty standing by the fire with a younger family she hadn't recognized.

Aunt Mary nudged Margaret while roasting a marshmallow over the fire. "Talk about Christmas miracles. Hugh and Betty's son and his family just showed up. We don't know how or why, but it seems to be a miracle alright."

Margaret smiled and looked over at Hugh and Betty. Betty had happy tears welling up in her eyes as she lifted her grandchild in her arms.

Just then, tiny, soft snowflakes fell from the sky, landing on the group as they sang and roasted marshmallows.

Margaret looked up at Dave. "You've done it again. Everything is so magical with you."

Dave smiled, and pulled her in for a close hug. "Merry Christmas, Margaret."

EPILOGUE

Liz blew a noisemaker towards Margaret and Sarah. Margaret laughed, grabbed one, and blew it back.

They were at the annual Silver and Gold New Year's Eve Ball in Cape May at an old, historic hotel. Dave, Greg, and Mark stood together at the bar across the room having a drink and chatting.

It was a black-tie event with women in floor-length ball gowns and men in black bow ties and tuxedo jackets. Silver and gold balloons littered the floor and covered the ceiling, candles lit every table.

The DJ slowed the music down, switching to a classic jazz song, and got on the microphone. "If everyone could take their seats, your servers will be by with the appetizers followed by dinner very shortly."

Sarah clapped her hands. "I'm so excited for dinner. They always outdo themselves with the food here."

"You're right. That filet mignon was exquisite last year. Remember the crème brûlée? I've never had a better one," Margaret said as she took a sip of her drink.

Dave, Greg, and Mark walked back over to the table, still chatting and laughing.

Margaret smiled. "What are you handsome guys talking about?"

Dave put his drink down and took his seat next to Margaret. "Oh, you know, how Greg wants to open a restaurant someday. He has a lot of details rolling around. Just has to take the plunge."

Greg smiled. "Yeah, I've been thinking about it for many years. My dad owned a restaurant growing up, and I have so many happy memories from that time. There's a lot I worry about, though. I've heard from friends who own restaurants that it will take over my life and drain me. There's also the finances and possible-failure aspect. It could put my family in the hole, or it could be an amazing success. Plus, Liz was supposed to open one with me, but with the B&B, I'm not sure how that would work."

Liz shrugged. "It could possibly work, but we'll have to wait and see."

Sarah piped in. "I'm actually thinking of opening a little coffee shop myself. It's been something I've pondered in the back of my mind for years and haven't told anyone about. Like you, Greg, I'm worried about finances and failure though."

Greg's face perked up and he held his glass up. "Well, cheers to our business ideas and figuring out if they're worth pursuing or not!"

The servers came by with three plates of different appetizers. There were little crab cakes, chicken lettuce wraps, and pear pecan toasts with blue cheese.

Liz took a bite of the crab cake and moaned. "You've got to be kidding me. How do they make everything taste so good?"

Sarah took a bite of the pear pecan toast. "Do you think they're holding the fort down at the B&B tonight?"

Margaret laughed. "Oh, definitely. I'm so glad we hired Kim and Dolly. They love working at the B&B and do such a good job. The guests absolutely adore them. It has given all of us a much-needed break, too."

Liz smiled. "I love that two sisters like us are also working at The Seahorse Inn."

Sarah coughed. "Wait, they're sisters? How did I not know this?"

Margaret laughed. "I guess we forgot to tell you. They're both retired, but called and inquired about working together a couple days a week at the B&B. They grew up going to the Seahorse and loved being there. We, of course, were happy to hire some part-time help."

Dinner was served next. They'd picked their meals months ago when they'd bought their tickets, but none of them could remember what they'd chosen.

Margaret was the first to be served a beautiful plate of scallops over risotto with charred corn.

Greg's eyes widened. "Man, I sure hope I picked that dish."

Dave grabbed a sneaky bite of Margaret's dish, and Margaret pinched him and laughed.

Liz received a grilled New York strip steak with smashed potatoes and asparagus. Everyone's eyes widened at how juicy and delicious it looked as they each eventually received their dinners and filled their bellies with the scrumptious food and drinks.

When a band took the stage and played 80s songs, Dave stood up and held his hand out to Margaret. "Come with me. Let's go burn off this dinner."

Margaret smiled, grabbed his hand, and let Dave lead her to the dance floor.

Liz and Sarah looked at Greg and Mark. "Well, let's do this! I want to dance!" Liz said as she got up directing everyone else to follow her to the dance floor.

They danced and danced all night. The DJ would play a set when the band went on break so there was nonstop music and dancing the entire evening.

Dessert was served, and they made their way back to the table, kicking off their shoes and getting comfortable.

On each of their table settings sat a plate of gourmet funnel cake pieces with homemade chocolate sauce to dip it in.

Liz laughed. "My boys would devour this in a second."

Sarah took a bite and started doing a happy fork dance. "You guys, this is not your average carnival funnel cake. Try it. It's amazing."

Moments later, Margaret's phone rang. "Oh, jeez. I hear my phone ringing. I hope Kim and Dolly are doing OK." She looked at her phone, which continued to ring and saw it was Dave's sister. "It's Irene. I wonder why she's calling me at eleven thirty on New Year's Eve," Margaret said.

Liz and Sarah looked at each other, shrugged and continued eating the funnel cake.

Holding the phone to her ear, Margaret silently mouthed to them that she was going to take the call outside where she could hear. "Hi, Irene. What's up?"

"Oh, hey, Margaret. Sorry to bother you, but I have some exciting news that I couldn't wait until tomorrow to tell you."

"Oh, what's that?" Margaret asked intrigued.

"Well, there's a big-budget film shooting in Cape May in February and March, and I've been asked to work on it," Irene said excitedly.

"Oh, that's wonderful, Irene! Congrats!" Margaret said.

Irene paused. "Thank you. Well, there's a few big celebrities who've been cast in the movie, and they'll need somewhere to stay. I recommended The Seahorse Inn to the producer at the meeting the other day, and he passed it along to Katherine Duffield's assistants."

Margaret gasped. "Wait, *the* Katherine Duffield? Possibly staying at our B&B? Are you serious?"

Irene laughed. "Oh, I'm dead serious. You may be getting a call from her assistant tonight."

Just then, Margaret's call waiting beeped. "Um, Irene, I

think they might be calling me right now. Let me call you back tomorrow."

"Sure thing, Margaret. Oh yeah, Happy New Year!"

Margaret answered the new call coming through. "Hello?"

A person on the other end seemed to be in a very loud room similar to the one Margaret had just walked out of.

"Hi, is this Margaret Wilder?"

Margaret could barely hear them over the music and yelled back. "Yes, it's Margaret."

"My name is Katie. I'm calling on behalf of Katherine Duffield. I'm her assistant. She will be shooting a movie in Cape May in February and March, and would like to book your entire B&B for that time period."

Margaret was in shock. This was the last thing she thought would happen at the Seahorse. Movies didn't shoot in Cape May all that often, especially with big-name celebrities.

"Yes! We would love that. Just text or e-mail me the exact dates," Margaret said as she paced in excitement outside.

The music got louder where Katie was. "Perfect. Well, I'd better be going. The ball is about to drop. I'll be in touch. Happy New Year!"

Margaret hung up and rushed back into the ball, excitement that she had no desire to hide plastered on her face.

She made it to the dance floor where everyone was standing with glasses in hand. Dave handed her her drink, put his arm around her just as the countdown to the new year started.

Ten … nine … eight … seven … six …

Liz and Sarah toasted with Margaret. "What did Irene want?" Liz asked quickly.

Five … four … three …

Margaret smiled. "Let's just say Katherine Duffield is shooting a movie here in February and March, and just asked to book the entire B&B for that time."

Two … one … Happy New Year!

* * *

Pick up **Book 3** in the Cape May Series**, Cape May Stars,** to follow Margaret, Liz, Greg, Dave, and some new characters as well as old familiar ones.

Sign up for my newsletter to keep up with new releases at **https://subscribepage.com/v8g919**

Follow me on Facebook at **https://www. facebook.com/ClaudiaVanceBooks**

ABOUT THE AUTHOR

Claudia Vance is a writer of women's fiction and clean romance. She writes feel good reads that take you to places you'd like to visit with characters you'd want to get to know.

She lives with her boyfriend and 2 cats in a charming small town in New Jersey, not too far from the beautiful beach town of Cape May. She worked behind the scenes on TV shows and film sets for many years, and she's an avid gardener and nature lover.

Made in the USA
Columbia, SC
03 October 2023

23844682R00079